CHRISTMAS WITH DADDY

BY
CJ CARMICHAEL

MILLS & BOON

First published in Great Britain 2009
Harlequin Mills & Boon Limited,
Eton House, 18-24 Paradise Road, Richmond, Surrey TW9 1SR

© Carla Daum 2008

ISBN: 978 0 263 87661 1

23-1209

Harlequin Mills & Boon policy is to use papers that are natural, renewable and recyclable products and made from wood grown in sustainable forests. The logging and manufacturing processes conform to the legal environmental regulations of the country of origin.

Printed and bound in Spain
by Litografia Rosés S.A., Barcelona

Nick Gray was the kind of guy smart mothers warned their daughters about.

After five years of living in the same neighbourhood, Bridget had seen Nick with so many different women, she'd given up asking their names.

Still, sometimes when Bridget looked at him, she felt a crazy, unfamiliar excitement. He made her aware of possibilities she would never normally consider. Possibilities that were neither safe nor sensible.

It took only a few seconds for her to shake off that feeling, though. Nick was drawn to glamour, sophistication and style. The women he dated turned heads on the sidewalk.

Just as well she wasn't Nick's type. She'd never been one for flirting and casual dating. Whereas even Nick's relationship with the woman he'd married had lasted less than a year.

It was an appalling record, and she ought to think less of Nick for it. But she couldn't help liking him, despite his rather obvious character flaws. Someone who loved his baby as much as he did couldn't

Hard to imagine a more glamorous life than being an accountant, isn't it? Still, **CJ Carmichael** gave up the thrills of income tax forms and double-entry book-keeping when she sold her first book in 1998. She has now written more than twenty-five novels and strongly suggests you look elsewhere for financial planning advice.

Deepest love to my mum, Kay Daum

Thanks To:
My writing friends
Brenda Collins, Donna Tunney and Sherile Reilly,
who sat around my dining-room table, talking and
brainstorming, as the Gray brothers came to life.

Pauline Edward
for sharing her expertise in numerology.

Constable Chris Terry
from the Calgary Police Department for once again
answering my questions about crime investigation. I'd
also like to thank his wife
(my hairstylist), Tracy, for introducing us
(and for many years of great haircuts)!

CHAPTER ONE

NICK GRAY'S BABY daughter, Mandy, was the cutest thing he'd ever seen. Too bad he didn't have a clue what to do with her.

She smiled adoringly at him from her seat in the stroller, showing off the two tiny teeth she'd sprouted this month. Flanking the stroller were a bulging suitcase and a pink diaper bag.

Pink.

Like he was going to carry *that* around.

His ex-wife stood behind all this, looking like a model in a sleek leather jacket and high-heeled boots. No one would guess Jessica had ever had a baby, let alone just six months ago.

"I can't do this," he said flatly. "You've never let me have Mandy overnight before. Now at the last minute, you expect me to take care of her full-time for three weeks?"

"I guess if the Hartford Police Department believes you're smart enough to be a detective, you ought to be able to handle a baby. I've written out everything you need to know in here."

She passed him a notebook, as well as another,

thicker book. "Plus, I'm lending you my copy of *What to Expect the First Year.* Don't lose it."

"Jessica—"

"Look, I'm not wild about leaving her with you, either. But this is a once-in-a-lifetime chance for me."

"Spending your Christmas vacation in Australia, compliments of an Aussie snowboarder you met on the slopes two weeks ago. Yeah, some *lifetime chance.*"

"Will is a great guy."

"I'm sure. Aren't they all?"

"You're a fine one to talk. What's the longest you've stuck with one girlfriend?"

"Let me see…nine months?"

Her face reddened and he knew he'd scored a point. "That doesn't count. You only married me because I was pregnant. We both knew it was a mistake almost right away."

"Wrong. *You're* the one who decided it was a mistake." When he'd said his vows, he'd intended to stick by them. Not that he and Jessica were such a perfect couple. But when you had kids, you stepped up to the plate.

It was what all the Gray men did. And while he couldn't live up to his older brothers in many other ways, in this one area he'd tried to do what was right.

"Don't give me that crap. You were relieved when I moved out. Even if you won't admit it." She pulled up the sleeve of her jacket so she could see the gold watch on her wrist. "We don't have time to argue. Will's picking me up for the airport in half an hour."

"Okay, so let's schedule our fight for when you get back. Is January fifth good for you?"

She ignored him, but he could tell she was struggling not to smile. Instead, she bent to whisper something to Mandy.

He heard snippets. "Mommy loves you…lots of presents…miss you, baby."

When she straightened, there were tears in her eyes. Not that he'd ever doubted that Jessica loved their daughter. But what kind of mother left her six-month-old baby while she cavorted with her new ski buddy in Australia?

"You're not listening to me. This really is a problem. I took today off, but I have to work tomorrow."

"Don't you have any vacation time coming?"

He grimaced. "Yeah, right." She knew he'd used it all in the weeks after Mandy was born. Besides, he'd just been promoted, assigned a new partner and given a high-profile case. "What am I supposed to do with Mandy while I'm on duty?"

"What all the rest of us working parents do, Nick. Hire a sitter. Or ask your mom."

He knew better than to mess with his mom's bridge/Scrabble/shuffleboard plans. Gavin and Allison would be the perfect choice. They were already looking after eight-year-old Tory and their new son, Jack. What was one more baby?

But his middle brother and his new wife lived in Squam Lake, New Hampshire. Much too far for a daily commute to Hartford.

Nick's head was still spinning with possibilities—

or rather the *lack* of them—when Jessica put a hand on his arm. He looked at her white-tipped fingernails with mild curiosity. Once, her touch had set his libido on fire. Now he felt nothing.

"Mandy has had her breakfast and her diaper is clean. In about two hours it will be time for her nap. Good luck, Nick. I'll check in with you after we land in Sydney."

And then she left.

Seconds ticked by. A minute passed. Silence.

Mandy's big eyes were fixed on him. She seemed expectant.

He turned his hands palms up. "Sorry kid. I have *no* idea what I'm doing here."

SINCE HE'D MADE detective and stopped shift work, Nick had fallen into a routine of spending Sunday afternoons with Mandy. The routine went like this:

Pick up Mandy after her nap. Strap her into the infant car seat that Gavin and Allison had bought him for a baby gift, then drive to Matthew and Jane's place.

Hand baby to either Mom, Jane or Matthew.

Grab a beer.

Watch TV, with intermittent interaction with baby.

At dinnertime, warm up the bottle and canned baby food that Jessica had packed in the diaper bag— yes, the ugly pink one.

Feed Mandy, then let his mom or Matt hold her while he ate his own dinner.

Get back in his car, drive to Jessica's and leave Mandy with her.

That was it. With the support of his extended family, he could look after his daughter for half a day maximum. How was he supposed to cope with her full-time? He loved holding Mandy close while she slept and trying to make her smile when she was awake. But he couldn't fill a day with that stuff. Not even when you factored in feedings, naps and changing diapers.

When she was older, they'd be able to go to the park, play board games and read books together. But Mandy was too little for any of that.

"You don't watch TV, do you?"

Mandy pursed her lips, blowing bubbles with her saliva.

"I didn't think so."

With Mandy still gazing intently at him, he pulled out Jessica's notebook. On the first page she'd listed emergency numbers: the doctor's office, the poison center, and several others.

He flipped the page to *Mandy's Daily Schedule*. His ex had itemized Mandy's routine, but when he read closely he realized the list wasn't very complete. For instance, at seven in the morning Mandy was supposed to be cleaned, dressed and fed.

Then there was nothing until her nap at ten.

That was two hours from now.

What was he supposed to do with a baby for two hours?

He looked at the *What to Expect* book, but it was too long. It would probably take him a couple hours to find the right chapter.

Nick smiled at his daughter. She smiled back. Maybe he wasn't supposed to do anything with the baby. Maybe she just sat in her stroller and looked at him while he went about his normal business.

Normal business for a day off work was reading the paper and enjoying a pot of coffee. Pleased with this idea, Nick wheeled the stroller to the kitchen, then started a pot. He spread the paper over the table, like usual, and got out his favorite mug.

Mandy whimpered.

He turned to look at her. "What was that?" The noise hadn't sounded like a cry. But it hadn't sounded happy, either. He pushed her stroller closer so she could keep her eyes on him. She seemed to like that for some reason.

He turned to the *City* section, looking to see if there was anything about the case he'd been assigned yesterday. He scanned the front page, then the rest of the section, but there was no mention of a runaway teenager.

Good.

Mandy made another noise. A little louder and longer than the last one. Definitely not happy. He pushed the stroller even closer. It didn't help. She screwed up her face and pushed out her bottom lip.

Clearly Mandy was not a fan of the coffee-and-newspaper routine.

Maybe he'd find something in her suitcase to distract her, but when he opened it, out tumbled clothes and more clothes. Nothing else.

He tried the diaper bag next. It was full of empty bottles, a tin of powder to make formula, jars of baby food and—rather unimaginatively—diapers. Again, there seemed to be enough of everything to last thirty days or more.

Finally he noticed the pocket on the back of the stroller. Great, here were some actual toys. He pulled them out, one by one, and passed them to Mandy. She just threw them on the floor—each one seemed to make her madder than the one before.

For Pete's sake, why hadn't Jessica bought the kid any toys that she liked?

"What's the matter, Mandy? Do you want some Hot Wheels? Maybe a Transformer?" He was pretty sure she was too young for those, though.

God, what was he going to do? The neighbors would soon be calling to complain. Besides, it kind of made his chest ache to see her acting so distressed.

Finally inspiration struck. He'd take her for a walk. There were always tons of parents and nannies pushing strollers around the neighborhood, even in the winter.

He bundled Mandy in her snowsuit again and just that seemed to be enough to distract her from crying. She stared at him with her big blue eyes, through a sheen of tears. When she finally smiled, it was like she'd never been unhappy at all.

"You like going for walks, don't you?" He dried her eyes with the corner of a flannel blanket, then grabbed his own coat and went out the door.

Fresh snow had fallen last night and as he pushed

the stroller down the sidewalk he was glad that back when they'd still been together, he and Jessica had decided to invest in one of those all-weather jogging strollers, even though neither one of them jogged. The big wheels cut through the powder like nobody's business.

He headed for the park.

Newly aware of babies, suddenly it seemed that he could see nothing but parents pushing babies in strollers or carrying them close to their chest in padded holders. Several of the mothers were rather pretty.

He caught the eye of a striking brunette walking toward him with her baby in a sling. She smiled and it occurred to him that she might be a single mother.

"Cute baby," she said. "Is that your daughter?"

"Yup." He could tell she wanted him to stop and talk. It would be so easy to do. He'd start by admiring her baby, then shift to a compliment about the mother's smile.

He kept walking.

Yummy mummies were fun to look at, but they weren't his style. Besides, since the breakup of his marriage, he'd been taking a little hiatus from women.

Nick ambled to the end of the street, then crossed to the park. To his right was a nicely maintained trail—the city even plowed off the snow in the winter.

He pushed the stroller, following the path along the river for a while until coming to a playground. A handful of kids were riding on the swings and scrambling over the monkey bars. Their mothers huddled on a park bench nearby, sipping from insulated coffee mugs and chatting.

Mandy sat forward in her seat, enchanted by the sight of the kids playing. She was too young to join them, of course, but he took her out of her stroller so she could have a better view.

She seemed fascinated.

But then she was equally intrigued by a handful of snow, an acorn, a dried-up brown leaf. Each treasure he presented to his young daughter seemed to fully occupy her senses until, finished exploring, she tossed the object to the ground.

Like the toys.

Now he understood. It wasn't that Mandy didn't like her toys. They bored her.

She was into new things. Learning about the world. And it was his job, as her parent, to make all the necessary introductions.

When he'd run out of things to show her, Nick put Mandy back into the stroller. He decided to take a fork in the path, going into an off-leash dog area in the woods. He pointed out a bird's nest exposed in a winter-bare tree, a chattering squirrel, rabbit tracks in the snow. Though she couldn't possibly understand, Mandy seemed to love it when he explained all this to her. She soaked in every new experience, waving her arms and babbling.

The off-leash route circled back to their starting point and as he was merging onto the main path, he heard dogs barking, then a sharp whistle. He turned and saw the neighborhood dog-sitter, Bridget

Humphrey, emerging from a curve in the path, with her pack of four dogs. She bent to pluck something from the graying Airedale's leg.

"Poor Stanley. Why do you always find the burrs? Stand still for a minute. There's a good boy."

As she dealt with Stanley's coat, three other dogs—a boxer, a white terrier and a giant schnauzer—circled her. When she was finished with Stanley, she clipped him back on the lead, then called the boxer closer.

He watched, impressed as always with the quiet authority she held over the dogs. He'd met Bridget on moving day when she'd brought over cookies to welcome him to the neighborhood. "We'll get along fine," she said, "as long as you don't mind dogs."

He loved dogs. Always had. One day he was going to break down and buy one himself. Bridget had already promised to make room in her doggy day care when he did.

Sometimes, when he happened upon Bridget and the dogs at the park, he walked along with them for a while. He enjoyed throwing sticks for them in the off-leash area and tussling on the grass when the weather was fine.

Bridget was just reaching for the collar of the schnauzer—Nick's favorite—when Herman spotted Nick. He gave one sharp bark of recognition, then set off running.

"Herman, stop!" Bridget called. Immediately the big gray dog jerked to a halt. He glanced over his shoulder at Bridget, then longingly toward Nick.

Nick had already positioned himself between the

dogs and his daughter. He'd seen them with kids before, knew they were gentle and well trained, but he wasn't taking chances.

Three seconds later, Bridget and the other dogs caught up to Herman. Bridget snapped the schnauzer onto the lead. "Sorry, Nick." She sounded breathless. "I should have put them back on leash sooner."

"No harm done." He held out a hand so the dogs could sniff. As he gave each dog a bit of attention, Bridget went to say hello to Mandy. His daughter was squirming with excitement.

"Can I take Mandy out of the stroller for a minute?"

"Sure." Herman nuzzled his hand, demanding more scratch time. As Nick complied, Bridget swung Mandy in the air, making her laugh.

"Oh, she's a sweetie, Nick. She wants to pet the dogs. Should I let her?"

"Sure."

Lefty, a sweet boxer who especially loved kids, approached and licked her little fingers. Mandy giggled.

"I think I've got a dog-lover on my hands," Nick said.

"Just like her dad." Bridget pushed her sunglasses up on her head and smiled at him.

He didn't often get a look at Bridget's eyes because she usually wore sunglasses. But when he did he was always startled that such a nondescript woman should have such gorgeous eyes. They were large and vibrantly green, like new leaves in the spring. Most intriguing of all, they slanted up at the edges, giving her ordinary face a mysterious allure.

"Not to be nosy," she said, "but why aren't you at work?"

"I booked the day off. My ex left for Australia today."

"Really? That's a big trip."

"Yeah, and she's going to be gone for three weeks." Which reminded him of his number-one problem. "Do you know of any good day cares in our neighborhood?"

"Sunny's Day Care is the best. But she has a six-month waiting list."

"Cripes. Any other suggestions?"

"What about your mom?"

"She's great with Mandy for an hour or two, but a whole day is out of the question. Have you heard about any other day cares?"

"Most of the good ones have waiting lists. Even *I* have a waiting list for new dogs."

"Yeah? How about babies? I don't suppose you could take on one of those?"

"You're not serious?"

"I don't know about serious. I am desperate, though."

She bit her bottom lip. Was she actually considering saying yes?

"I'd pay you well. And it's only for three weeks." He hesitated, suddenly wondering if she could handle the job. Babies were a bit more complicated than dogs. "Have you looked after a baby before?"

"I worked at a day care one summer when I was in college," she offered reluctantly.

So she was experienced. Even better. "I'll pay you double the going rate."

"Mandy's a sweetheart, Nick, but these guys keep me pretty busy." She gave the end of her leash a gentle tug. "Plus I have my business appointments, too."

The dogs were really a sideline with Bridget. Her main occupation was as a numerology and astrology consultant. He had a hard time taking that stuff seriously, but he knew she did. Generally avoiding the subject seemed to work best.

"Mandy wouldn't be that much trouble. Plus, she loves going on walks. You can take her with the dogs. She'll fit right in."

"I'm sure she wouldn't be *trouble,* but…"

"Besides, couldn't you use some extra cash for Christmas? For gifts and things?"

"I don't need extra money."

"You're not giving me much to bargain with." If she was any other woman, he might try charming her with a smile, but he couldn't see that approach working with Bridget. Every now and then he came across a woman who was impervious to his brand of sex appeal. From their first meeting his instincts had told him that Bridget was one of those women.

Still, he had to come up with something. He was due at the station tomorrow at eight in the morning. And he didn't think his partner was expecting him to bring along his six-month-old daughter.

CHAPTER TWO

NICK GRAY WAS THE KIND of guy smart mothers warned their daughters about. After five years of living in the same neighborhood, Bridget had seen him with so many different women, she'd given up asking their names. In the historical novels she loved, he was the rake, the ne'er-do-well but handsome younger brother, the favorite son who always disappointed his father but was the apple of his mother's eye.

Sometimes when Bridget looked at him, she felt a crazy, unfamiliar excitement. He made her aware of possibilities that she would never normally consider. Possibilities that were neither safe nor sensible.

It only took a few seconds for her to shake off that feeling, though. Nick was drawn to glamour, sophistication and style. The women he dated turned heads on the sidewalk. And not because they had four dogs in tow.

Just as well she wasn't Nick's type. She'd never been one for flirting and casual dating. Whereas even Nick's relationship with the woman he'd married had lasted less than a year.

It was an appalling record, and she ought to think

less of Nick for it. But she couldn't help liking him, despite his rather obvious character flaws. Someone who loved dogs as much as he did, couldn't be all bad.

He had a special affinity for her giant schnauzer Herman. Aptly named, Herman was solid, dependable, unstoppable when he wanted something. And when Nick was around, there was no doubt what Herman wanted.

She couldn't blame him.

"I know I'm asking a lot," Nick said. "It's okay if you'd rather not do it."

Now she felt guilty. Nick was a good neighbor and a friend, too. They collected each other's mail when they went on vacations. Occasionally Nick helped her out with the dogs. Just last month when she'd been sick with the flu, he'd taken them all for a long run at the end of his shift.

But babies required a lot more time and effort than dogs.

Nick gave Herman one last scratch, then he stood and reached for Mandy. His baby daughter held out her arms to him, smiling as he drew her close.

They looked so cute together. Gosh, a guy who was good with dogs *and* babies. It just wasn't fair. How was any woman supposed to resist *that?*

Then suddenly, for no apparent reason, Mandy started to cry. Nick's face registered surprise as he glanced at Bridget, then back at the baby.

"Hey, what's wrong, sweetie?"

Mandy's cries grew louder. The dogs pulled in close to Bridget. The baby's distress made them uneasy.

"Do you know what time it is?" Nick asked. "I forgot to put on my watch this morning."

She shrugged. She hadn't worn a watch, either. "Almost one o'clock," she guessed. She and the dogs had left the house at eleven-thirty and the route through the woods usually took them about an hour and a half.

"One o'clock." Nick seemed astounded. "I didn't think we'd been out that long. Mandy missed her nap *and* her lunch."

No wonder she was so upset. "Did you bring any food with you?"

"It didn't occur to me. Maybe Jessica packed something in here...." Nick rummaged through the storage pouch on the back of the stroller but came up with nothing. Mandy was sobbing now, and for a guy who never seemed to lose his cool, Nick was looking pretty flustered.

"What should I do? I've got to get her home, but I can't put her in the stroller when she's crying like this."

"I'll push the stroller for you." Bridget tied the dogs' leads to the handle, then started along the path at a fast clip.

Nick fell in next to her. "Thanks a lot. I guess I should have been more prepared." He cuddled Mandy closely. "Don't worry, honey. Your dad's an idiot, but he *is* going to feed you, eventually."

As they made their way out of the park area onto the city streets, Bridget noticed they were attracting quite a bit of attention. A man and a woman with four dogs and a crying baby...yeah, she wasn't too surprised people were gawking.

Nick seemed oblivious to the stares, though. He was almost panicking by the time they reached his town house. "Will you come inside?"

She didn't have the heart to leave him to cope alone. "What about the dogs?"

"I have a fenced backyard. Will that do?"

"I'll need to give them some water."

"Not a problem."

He dug into his pocket for the keys, and then, she was in a place she never thought she'd see the inside of—Nick Gray's town house. She wasn't sure what she'd expected. Maybe sleek furniture, an opulent TV and sound system...a round bed with satin sheets?

But his furnishings were plain and sparse. He had just one reclining chair in his living room, along with the television. In the kitchen down the hall, a newspaper was spread over a tiny oak table. Two folding chairs sat around it.

Nick must have noticed her scrutinizing the place because he apologized. "Jessica took a lot of stuff when she moved out. I haven't been in the mood to replace it."

He paused, frowning. "Is something burning? Hell. I forgot to turn off the coffee machine." Still carrying Mandy, whose crying had turned into pitiful hiccups, he crossed the room and hit the off button on the coffeemaker. Then he grabbed a big bowl from a cupboard and handed it to her.

"For the dogs." He pointed to the patio door. "You can let them out there."

"Thanks." She unlocked the door then released the

dogs from their leashes. They rushed outside, anxious to explore. Once she had filled the bowl with water and placed it on the patio for them, she went to check on Nick.

He was kneeling on the kitchen floor, holding Mandy in one hand and pulling stuff out of a pink diaper bag with the other.

He cursed softly. "Couldn't she have prepared one bottle at least?" He found a can of powder. "Jessica mixes some of this with water. I have no idea about the ratio."

"Instructions should be on the can. How about I read them while you get Mandy out of her snowsuit. She must be very warm."

A guilty look crossed his face. "Good thinking." He unzipped Mandy's snowsuit and for a couple of peaceful moments the baby actually stopped crying. But as he stripped off the cute yellow snowsuit, he made a face. "Oh-oh."

Bridget glanced up from the fine print on the can. "What's wrong?"

"She's soaking wet. She needs a bath and a new diaper. God, I am *such* an imbecile."

And then, as if to signal her agreement, Mandy started howling again.

ONE HOUR LATER Mandy had been bathed, changed, fed and lulled to sleep, in that order. Bridget did most of the work, with Nick watching, feeling like he was on the verge of having a heart attack.

Now, seeing Mandy's peaceful face, her body

curled under the flannel covers, he could finally take a deep, long breath.

"Thank you, Bridget."

She was on the other side of the crib, looking at him with an odd smile. "You're welcome."

"You made it all seem easy."

"It's not so difficult. You just need to stay calm."

Calm. That was funny. "I've given that same advice to rookie cops in dangerous situations on the street. I can keep my head when a robbery is going down. But babies are different."

"You'll catch on," Bridget said gently.

"You think?"

"You've definitely got potential. As long as you don't panic, you'll be able to handle Mandy just fine."

He wished he had the same faith in himself that she did. "I'll still need a sitter for when I'm at work."

Bridget broke eye contact. "I should get going."

"Oh, no. You're not leaving until you agree to take on the job. You've just proved you're the perfect person to take care of Mandy."

The prospect of extra money hadn't tempted her. What would motivate someone like her? "Please, Bridget? We've been neighbors for years and Mandy already likes you. I'd hate to have to leave her with a stranger."

"Not fair, Nick." She shook her head at him. "But I will do it. If you're willing to make a few compromises."

Years of negotiating with two older brothers had made him cautious. "Yeah?"

"We do this the ecofriendly way. That means organic, homemade baby food, no disposable bottle liners, and definitely no more disposable diapers."

"You want me to use cloth diapers?"

She nodded.

"God, Bridget." Cloth diapers would be stinky. And they'd have to be washed. "Okay. But you better be worth it."

OH, I AM, Bridget wanted to say. *I am definitely worth it.*

But she wouldn't be talking about babysitting. She'd be *flirting*. And where that urge had come from, she wasn't sure. The situation was far from romantic. They were talking about baby food and diapers for heaven's sake.

The problem was Nick. If only he had the good grace to look like a respectable father. But no, even in a domesticated scene like this one, he still exuded sex appeal.

Even as she was thinking about that, he stood up and stretched out his arms, inadvertently flexing all sorts of lovely muscles for her to admire.

She shouldn't be looking. What she should be doing was leaving. "I'd better round up my dogs and get home."

"I'll call them in." As soon as Nick slid open the patio door, all four of the snowy canines barreled inside. Bridget apologized, but Nick didn't seem too worried about the floor getting wet.

As she clipped the dogs onto their leashes, Nick's

phone rang. After his first few responses, she was amazed by the change that came over him.

Her charming, light-hearted neighbor was suddenly serious and focused. He listened intently, then said, "You bet. Twenty minutes."

After he hung up, he tunneled his fingers through his thick dark hair, then looked at her with a speculative gleam in his eye.

Oh, boy. "What is it?" she asked cautiously.

"I'm working on this case right now. A runaway teenager. She's only fourteen."

"That's young," she said.

"By all accounts she's a good kid, from a good family. We'd like to find her as quickly as possible, for a lot of reasons, not the least because the streets aren't exactly a safe place for someone like her."

She nodded, agreeing, and understanding his urgency.

"We had a possible sighting at the mall in West Hartford. My partner's not available, so I'd like to check it out."

"Now?" Why was she asking? Of course he had to go now. "I can stay for a while, but I have to be home by quarter to five. Foster's owner usually picks him up around then."

Nick's taut features relaxed with relief. "Thank you, Bridget. You're amazing."

Amazing. Nick Gray thought she was amazing. Of course she knew he meant this in a platonic, thanks-for-helping-me-out-in-a-pinch way, but still it was nice to hear.

He went to his bedroom and came out wearing a holster strapped to his chest. She did her best not to stare at this visible reminder of the dangers of his job. Noticing his keys on the floor by the front door, she picked them up and passed them to him.

Bridget was struck again by the domesticity of the situation. This must be what it would be like to be married to a cop. Only, if they were married, Nick would be kissing her goodbye right now…

Right. Dream on, Bridget. You're the babysitter, not the girlfriend.

"Thanks, Bridget. Here's one of my new business cards. Call my cell if you need me."

He'd told her last month about his promotion. She glanced at the card before slipping it into her pocket. "Thanks, Detective."

He gave her a boyish grin, full of self-conscious pride. "Yeah, I'm a bigwig now. You remember that."

"I'm impressed. But I still need to be home by four forty-five."

He nodded.

"You won't be late?"

"I won't be late."

NICK WAS late. But it was only by five minutes. She'd give him another five, Bridget decided, before she panicked.

Mandy had woken half an hour ago and Bridget had changed her diaper and given her something to drink. Now Mandy was sitting on the floor next to Lefty. The boxer had befriended the baby, not seeming to mind at all when Mandy pulled his ears or poked at his whiskers.

The other dogs were still sleeping, worn-out by the long walk and the romp in Nick's backyard. Herman was on the floor by Nick's recliner, while Stanley and Foster were settled on the rug by the front door. Clearly they weren't going to be left behind when it came time to leave.

Earlier, she'd found an old towel and used it to dry the pads on the dogs' feet, then the puddles on the kitchen floor. And she'd cleaned up the mess she and Nick had made in the kitchen preparing Mandy's lunch.

Now with the baby happily distracted by Lefty, Bridget had nothing to do. There were bookshelves next to the television. Maybe she should find something to read. Framed photographs next to the books distracted her, though. She found one of Nick and two other men who had to be his brothers.

Nice-looking guys, all of them, with thick dark hair and likable grins. But to her, only Nick had that special something. A sparkle in his eyes, a certain slant to his grin. She'd bet he had been a handful as a little boy.

There were other photos, too. One of an older woman—probably Nick's mom. She had the same light blue eyes…like the sky on a cold winter day.

Bridget caught her breath when she noticed a wedding photo of Nick and Jessica. Oh my Lord, his wife had made such a beautiful bride. What would it be like to be that gorgeous?

When she was younger, Bridget had often despaired of her own wiry red hair and plain features. But not anymore. Being pretty didn't guarantee a woman love and happiness. Wasn't Jessica the perfect example of that? She and Nick may have looked like a Hollywood couple on their wedding day, but they'd never even celebrated their first anniversary.

Bridget moved on to the next shelf, which had been dedicated to chronicling the first six months of Mandy's life. She smiled at the image of Mandy as a newborn, in her father's arms. Nick looked happy but nervous.

He still seemed a little nervous around his daughter. Maybe this three-week vacation of his ex-wife's was a blessing in disguise. He needed time to get comfortable with his new role as father.

She would help him with that.

As soon as she had the thought, she realized she was overreaching. Nick's competence as a father wasn't any of her business. Looking after Mandy didn't change the nature of their relationship. They were neighbors. Good neighbors who looked out for one another and offered a hand, when needed.

Nothing else.

Bridget paced the main floor, as anxious as Lefty during a thunderstorm. Nowhere did she see any preparations for Christmas. No tree, no wrapping paper, no decorations.

Guys without families probably didn't bother with those things. But Nick had a family now. Surely he'd want his daughter's first Christmas to be special. Maybe she should suggest…

Oh, Lord, she was doing it again. Getting too involved. How Nick decided to spend the holidays with his daughter was none of her business, either.

The dogs. They were her business. She glanced at her watch. Five more minutes had passed. Still no sign of Nick.

Okay, now it was time to panic.

CHAPTER THREE

BRIDGET WAS ROUTED to messages on Nick's cell phone. "It's almost five," she said. "If you're not home in two minutes I'm taking Mandy to my place."

She picked up the baby and coaxed a smile from her. It wasn't hard to do. Mandy really was a doll. Obviously Lefty thought so, too. The boxer looked up at Bridget mournfully, as if to say, *why did you have to take her away?*

Bridget bundled Mandy into her snowsuit again, then settled her into the stroller cautiously. To her relief Mandy was perfectly happy to go on another outing.

Still, Bridget was not impressed. If Nick thought he could flash his sexy grin at her and get away with stunts like this, he was sorely mistaken.

NICK HAD BEEN PROMOTED to detective four weeks ago, and he loved it. He loved being able to dress in plain clothes and drive an unmarked car. He loved working regular hours instead of shifts and having his weekends free the majority of the time.

He especially loved the challenge of working on cases and feeling he was actually making a difference.

When he reached the mall, he parked and took out the photo he had of the missing girl. Tara Lang smiled up at him, her large brown eyes full of defiance.

Clearly she hadn't wanted to pose for this photo. Who had taken it, he wondered? One of her parents, perhaps?

Fourteen years from now, would Mandy look at him like this if he tried to take her picture? He sure hoped not.

A group of kids were hanging out around the benches by the mall entrance, probably waiting for rides from their parents. He studied them as he passed by, but none of them came close to matching Tara's description.

Once inside he headed for the food court, where Tara had supposedly been spotted. He circled the area, passing Japanese eateries, burger spots, smoothie joints and taco stalls, stopping frequently to show the picture and ask if anyone had seen the girl.

No luck.

He hadn't really expected it to be this easy, but he'd hoped. Solving this case would be a great way to begin his career as an investigator, since the Chief had made it clear that this case was the number-one priority of the entire department.

Nick went over every corridor of the mall, twice, before finally conceding defeat. As he headed for his parked car, his mind was full of thoughts about Tara Lang. He wondered where she was right now. Was she safe with friends?

Or out on her own?

Was she still defiant and angry at her parents? Or was she scared and sorry she'd run away?

Then there was the worst possibility of all. That she'd been the victim of a crime. Kidnapped, assaulted or even…

No. He wasn't going there. Not yet. She hadn't been missing more than twenty-four hours. Her father believed she was hiding out with one of her friends. Hopefully he was right.

As he slid into the driver's seat, Nick's focus settled on the time display. Cripes, was it five o'clock already?

Where had the time gone? He opened a window and slapped a siren on the roof of the car. God, Bridget was going to be totally pissed at him.

ONLY AFTER HE'D ARRIVED home and found the place deserted did Nick think to check his messages. As he listened to Bridget's recording he noticed she'd also left her business card on his kitchen table. *Pampered Pooches…loving care for your best friend.*

He stared at the slogan for a moment. He knew, firsthand, that it wasn't an idle claim. Bridget did give loving care to all of her dogs. She had a big, generous heart and he'd taken advantage of that today when he'd convinced her to help him with Mandy.

And now he was late. Not a good first impression.

Using a magnet, he stuck the card to his fridge, then jogged out to the street. Bridget lived just two doors down in an identical town house to all the others on this block. But she'd managed to make her place stand out thanks to her mailbox, which had been built and painted to look like a miniature doghouse.

A dusting of snow covered the sidewalk that led to her door and he could see the tracks of Mandy's stroller, several sets of boot prints, and lots of doggy paws leading up and down the stairs. He added his footprints to the mix, hurrying to the door, then knocking.

As he waited he noticed two discreet brass placards screwed to the wall just under the outdoor lamp. *Pampered Pooches* and *Bridget Humphrey, Numerologist.*

He cringed at the second one, just as the door was whisked open.

"About time." She sounded annoyed.

"I'm sorry. I should have called—"

Bridget nodded. "No kidding. Nick, if this arrangement is going to work, you need to respect my schedule and my time. I have commitments, too, you know."

He apologized again. "I just couldn't resist a second look around the mall."

Bridget's face softened. "You didn't find her?"

"No."

"I'm sorry. I hope she's all right." She stepped back from the door. "Come on in. Mandy's just had her bottle and now she's playing with my yarn basket."

The house smelled...tantalizing. Like oatmeal cookies, he decided as he removed his boots and looked around. The rooms were laid out the same as his, but the similarity between the two homes ended there.

Bridget had put her stamp on this place, made it warm and inviting. The living room was alive with colors and textures, including a fluffy white rug. Mandy sat plum in the center of it, surrounded by dozens of balls of yarn, each one a different color.

He didn't need to see Mandy's smile to know that she was loving this. "She's discovering the world."

Bridget looked at him as if he'd said something clever. "That's right. She is."

As soon as she spotted him, Mandy held out her arms and smiled. In his mind, he imagined her one year older saying "Daddy! Daddy!" the way he remembered his nieces doing for his brother Gavin when he came home from work.

He swung her up, then hugged her. He was surprised by the feelings that swamped him, even though he'd last seen her only a few hours ago. It was almost as if he were choking on one of those balls of yarn. He swallowed, then turned to Bridget. "I'm really sorry I was late. I didn't want to leave the mall until I was sure the runaway wasn't there."

Bridget didn't seem angry anymore. "Tell me about this girl. You said she was a good kid from a nice family. Why did she run away?"

Mandy reached for the yarn and he set her back down amid the colored balls. "According to her father, there were some typical teenage rebellion issues. Unfair curfews, too many family functions, not enough time for friends. He said they had a big argument on Tuesday night. Wednesday morning, when she didn't come down for breakfast, his wife checked her room and found her gone."

"Did she go to a friend's house? That's what I would have done."

Nick felt a flash of curiosity. Had Bridget suffered from rebellion issues in *her* youth? Surely not. She didn't look the type. "That's exactly what her parents assumed she'd done. But when they hadn't heard anything by the next morning they became worried. Yesterday the mother questioned all of her daughter's friends, but no one had seen her."

"Could they be covering for their friend?"

"It's certainly possible. In fact, I hope that's what's happened. It beats the alternatives."

"An abduction…"

He nodded. "Her father is an important political official here in Hartford. So kidnapping is a possibility. Though we aren't considering it likely since the girl's warmest coat, her backpack, wallet, iPod and cell phone are all missing."

"So she probably ran away."

"It definitely looks that way. What happened after she hit the streets though…" He shrugged. "Hartford isn't Detroit, but every city has its criminal elements. A girl on her own could get into trouble pretty quickly." Especially a girl with no street smarts.

"Maybe she left Hartford?"

"We don't think so. She's too young to drive, and we're keeping tabs on the bus station and airport. It's possible she hitched a ride from a stranger, but again, that doesn't seem likely."

"Her poor family." She tilted her head and eyed

him speculatively. "I'd be happy to try and help you. All you'd need to do is tell me this girl's full name and birth date."

He didn't understand the reason for her question at first. Then he scowled. "Are you talking about numerology?"

"Don't sound so skeptical. Numbers are all around us, and they have power and meaning."

"Get real. This kid's name and birth date isn't going to tell us where she is."

"Did I say they would? What numerology *will* do is give us some insight into what's in this girl's head right now. Where her life is leading her."

"Yeah, well, thanks for the offer. But I think I'll conduct this investigation the traditional way."

"Lots of intelligent, educated people believe in numerology, Nick. It's not that strange. If you'd like a demonstration, I'd be happy to show you. Give me *your* birth date."

He looked at her suspiciously.

"Let me calculate your life path number."

"What the heck is a life path number?"

"It's like a road map for your life, highlighting the opportunities and challenges that you'll face in your journey through this world. The life path number is the cornerstone of numerology."

Did she have any idea how wacko she sounded? "Look, I'm sure this is interesting to a lot of people. I just happen to put my faith in things that are more objective. Like the size of bullets, the patterns of fingerprints and the results of DNA testing."

"Okay. Fine. Forget it. Clearly you haven't evolved to this level yet."

Evolved. Right. That was one way of putting it. Still, nutty as he thought this numerology stuff was, he didn't want to insult her.

He inhaled deeply. "Look, I realize lots of people check their horoscopes every day. I'm just not one of them. And I don't base my police work on the stars—or numbers, either."

"Maybe so far you haven't. But later, if it turns out you do need my help, don't let pride stand in the way of asking for it."

He almost laughed. Fat chance of that happening.

CHAPTER FOUR

BECAUSE BRIDGET'S DAYS were busy with the dogs, she saw most of her numerology clients during the evening. This worked well for her clients, too, who juggled their timetables around the demands of work and family life.

Bridget ate a tofu stir-fry for dinner, then went to her office and spent an hour charting. At ten minutes to eight, she put water on to boil. She had tea steeping in an antique pot and two cups at the ready in her office when the doorbell rang.

Annabel Lang was a beautiful woman in her late thirties. Today she wore a trendy sweat suit, the kind that only looked good if you were a size six or smaller.

"Hi, Annabel. Come in."

Annabel managed only a brief, tense smile. She'd sounded upset on the phone and Bridget led her to the office, concerned that something serious must be wrong.

"Sit down and make yourself comfortable. Would you like tea?"

"Yes, thank you."

Annabel had been coming to Bridget for numerological readings ever since she'd heard Bridget speak at a workshop on goal-setting two years ago. Like many of her clients, Annabel was a planner. Someone who thought about her future and wanted as much information as she could get in order to make the best decisions for herself and her family.

She was also struggling with a marriage that was far from ideal. With the help of numerology she was trying to see the bigger patterns in her life as a way to guide her through these rough patches.

"Last night you said you wanted to talk about your daughter."

"Yes."

"Okay." Bridget pulled out the cover sheet of the report she'd prepared. "Let's start with Tara's life path number. I see your daughter as having an overabundance of nine energy in her life. This would make her somewhat naive for her age, highly emotional and unrealistic."

Annabel nodded vehemently. "So true. Can you tell me what might be on her mind right now?"

"I see her feeling isolated and not necessarily comfortable sharing her feelings."

Annabel shielded her eyes for a moment, then sighed. "That's an understatement. In the past year she's become so withdrawn. It's all I can do to get her to the dinner table for a meal. As soon as she's finished eating, she scurries back to her room."

"Yet what she longs for most right now is probably love."

Tears shimmered in Annabel's eyes. "I have plenty of that for her. But she doesn't let me in."

"It's partly her age, but partly who she is. Tara's looking for love, Annabel, but I don't think it's from her parents. I don't even think it's from her peers."

As Bridget read through the rest of her analysis, Annabel seemed to become increasingly restless. Finally Bridget had to stop. "Is something wrong?"

"No. It's just that I'm so worried about my daughter right now. And what you're saying...I'm afraid it isn't very reassuring."

"Is there something specific you'd like to talk about?"

"Yes. But I can't. I promised my husband." She stopped to gather her composure. "Bridget, are you free later this week? I may need to talk to you again."

"Of course." Much as she wanted to help right now, Bridget didn't press for more information. This was Annabel's life, Annabel's child. When the time was right, Annabel would let her know what was going on. Perhaps Tara was involved with a boy her parents considered inappropriate. Given her profile, maybe someone older. Certainly the signs pointed in that direction.

ACCORDING TO Jessica's schedule, Mandy went to bed at eight o'clock. Tonight, however, Mandy seemed to have other ideas.

Nick had followed Jessica's instructions to the letter, feeding Mandy dinner, giving her a bath, putting on her sleepers, then finally offering a bedtime bottle before laying her into the crib in the spare room.

Mandy had slept in that crib before she and Jessica had moved out.

But tonight, every time he tried to settle her there, she started to cry. Was she missing her mother and her familiar bedroom? Nick had no idea. As ten o'clock approached and Mandy's blue eyes remained wide open and alert, he started to feel desperate.

Whenever he picked her up, she'd start to relax. Her breathing would slow and her eyes would droop. But put her down in the crib? No way.

"Daddy can't hold you all night long, honey. Daddy needs to go to work tomorrow."

Mandy just stared at him.

Nick paced for another half hour. Finally, when he was certain Mandy was sound asleep, he eased her into her bed. Yes! She was still sleeping. He covered her with the flannel blankets, then tiptoed for the door…

Before he'd made it to the hall, Mandy was crying again. He pressed his head to the door frame and froze in place. Maybe if he gave her a few minutes…

But she only cried harder and, after five minutes, he couldn't take it anymore.

"Okay, baby, it's okay." He rescued her from the crib and held her to his chest. Immediately she calmed.

It was almost eleven now and he was more tired than usual for some reason. He needed to hit the sack. Maybe one of his brothers could help. They'd both been through this before.

Nick grabbed the phone and hit Gavin's speed dial number. His brother sounded as if he'd been sleeping.

"Sorry to call so late, but I'm desperate." He explained the situation. "Do you think she's sick or something?"

"If she's eating okay and it doesn't feel like she's running a fever, probably not." Gavin yawned audibly, then added, "Most babies like routine. It's probably going to take Mandy a while to get used to sleeping at your place again. If I was you, I'd expect a few restless nights."

"That's it? That's the best you can offer me?"

"Just make her feel safe, bro. Comfort her. Hold her close and sing to her."

"I've been doing that, man." And it wasn't working. He'd thought his brother would be more helpful than that.

Around midnight, Mandy started fussing, even when he was holding her, even when he tried singing one of the songs on her lullaby CD.

Nothing he said, or did, seemed to soothe her. He tried warming another bottle. She wanted nothing to do with it. Her fussing turned into sobbing.

Finally, when it was almost one in the morning, Nick decided to try the one thing that hadn't let him down so far. He bundled his daughter into her snowsuit, strapped her into the stroller, swaddled a bunch of blankets around her, then wheeled her outside.

Mandy instantly grew quiet.

The winter night was magical. Snow fell softly,

the crystals glittering like suspended diamonds under the streetlamps. His boots and the tires of the stroller crunched as he moved forward. Street traffic was minimal and in the silence he could hear the steady inhale, exhale of his breath.

Nick pushed the stroller up and down the block. Thankfully he didn't see anyone he knew. They'd think he was nuts.

He thought he was nuts.

Yawning again, he retraced his route, waiting for Mandy to fall asleep. It didn't take long to happen. The next time he checked, her cherry lips were parted ever so slightly and her eyes were closed.

He went up and down the block two more times to be certain, then rolled the stroller back inside his town house. Quietly he removed his jacket and boots, then looked down at his sleeping daughter.

She looked so peaceful. He felt a bone-deep sense of satisfaction until he realized he had a problem.

How the hell was he supposed to move her from the stroller to her crib? He just knew that as soon as he tried, she'd wake up and start crying again.

After a moment's consideration, he wheeled the stroller into his bedroom. Staring down at her, he wondered if she was going to get too warm with all those blankets, plus the snowsuit. He removed a few blankets, unzipped her snowsuit and removed her mittens.

What else should he do?

Frankly, he had no idea.

He collapsed on his bed and fell asleep himself.

USUALLY NICK AWOKE to the six-o'clock news on the local radio station. Not this morning though.

An obnoxious sound had him cramming his pillow around his head and over his ears. Why the hell didn't those people do something about their kid?

And then it hit him.

The crying was from *his* kid.

His eyes opened and he jerked upright. Blankets were rustling in the stroller. Once he'd flipped on the bedside lamp, he could see Mandy's face, red and angry. She flailed her little fists at the sight of him, as if to say, *Don't just stand there. Do something, Daddy!*

He picked her up and she was quiet. With her bundled next to his chest, he went to the living room where he'd left Jessica's notebook. For about the tenth time that night, he checked her instructions.

Eight o'clock, put Mandy to bed. She should sleep through until six or seven the next morning. He checked the time—it was only three!

Why hadn't Jessica written any instructions about what to do if Mandy woke up this early?

Should he feed her breakfast? Offer her another bottle? Try to lull her back to sleep?

He was sorely tempted to call Bridget and ask what she thought. Though she had no children of her own, she seemed to instinctively know how to deal with babies. But to call her at three in the morning…he might be pushing his luck just a little if he did that.

He lifted Mandy until her face was right next to his. "It's *early,* sweetheart. You're supposed to be sleeping right now." They were *both* supposed to be sleeping right now.

He put on the lullaby CD, but again, it was useless. Mandy seemed fine as long as he was holding her. A few times her eyes drooped shut…but as soon as he tried to lay her in the crib she started crying.

After forty-five minutes, he finally gave in to the inevitable and strapped her back into the stroller.

Outside, another inch of snow had fallen. He felt the thick flakes brush against his face as he headed to the far end of the block, then back. He did this four times. A man exited a town house on the opposite side of the street. He gave Nick a long look but said nothing, then continued to his car.

Remembering his own years of shift work, Nick felt a moment's sympathy for the guy. Then he shook his head. Was he crazy? *He* was the one who deserved the sympathy tonight.

It was past four when Nick's head finally hit his pillow for the second time that night. He could have sworn only five minutes had passed when suddenly his favorite news lady was talking about political developments in the Middle East.

Forget that. He pounded on the snooze button to shut her up. But he was too late.

Mandy started to cry.

AT HER FIRST SIGHT of him the next morning, Bridget could tell Nick had had an uneasy night with Mandy. He looked terrible. Eyes red, face badly shaven, his hair as rumpled as the shirt beneath his unzipped jacket. She opened the door wide to make room for the stroller. Nick was also carrying the pink diaper bag and another black vinyl bag.

"It's a portable crib," he explained, as she took it out of his hands with raised eyebrows. "So Mandy has a place to take her naps. Assuming she'll sleep for you, that is."

He slipped out of his boots and pushed the stroller into the living room. Glancing around, he asked, "Where are the dogs?"

"Out back, romping in the new snow." She deposited the bag with the crib near the doorway to the spare room. "How did things go last night?"

"Terrible."

"What happened?"

"Mandy didn't go to sleep until one in the morning. Then she was awake from three to four." He picked up his daughter, then extricated her from the snowsuit with the expertise of one who had done the same task many, many times before.

Mandy smiled winningly, then held out her arms to Bridget. "Hey, sweetie." Bridget scooped her up. She smelled clean and looked happy.

"I just changed her diaper," Nick confirmed. "And she's had her breakfast...unlike me."

The last two words were spoken so quietly Bridget didn't think she'd been meant to hear them. "I baked muffins this morning. Would you like a couple?"

His face brightened. "That's what smells so good in here."

Hoisting Mandy to a hip, she headed for the kitchen.

Nick followed. "How do single parents cope? I doubt I had five hours of sleep last night. And this morning I had to rush through my shower and didn't even have time to shave properly." He rubbed the side of his face and shook his head.

Bridget watched him, fighting an urge to touch the other side of his face with her free hand. He did look rough this morning, she had to agree.

But on Nick Gray, rough wasn't bad. Not bad at all.

She put two muffins into a plastic bag, then added an apple. "You can eat on the way to work. And don't worry about Mandy. I'll take good care of her."

"I know you will. Thanks, Bridge."

Bridge? Normally she hated it when people shortened her name that way. But coming from Nick, it sounded good. Friendly…almost intimate.

"You okay?" Nick's voice held a touch of concern. "You got a strange look on your face for a second there."

"I'm *fine*," she said. "Now you better hurry and get to work." *And get out of my sight so I stop fantasizing about you.*

"Okay."

She thought he was leaving, but instead he moved closer. So close that Bridget's heart stopped. Good Lord, it was almost as if he intended to—

"Bye-bye, Mandy." He lowered his head, his hair brushing against Bridget's nose as he planted a kiss on his daughter's cheek.

Bridget inhaled the scent of his shampoo. *Kiss me, too,* she couldn't help wishing, even as she had the good sense to step back.

"I'll see you around five," Nick promised on his way out the door.

Bridget moved to the kitchen window and watched as he headed toward his car. She was willing to bet he was a good athlete. He was so sure-footed and confident in the way he moved. A man who knew where he was going and what he wanted.

What would it be like to be the sort of woman that Nick Gray was attracted to?

Over the years she'd often wondered that, experiencing a touch of envy for the girlfriends she'd seen dangling from his arm. A harmless crush was what she'd called these yearnings for her appealing neighbor. She'd never imagined that one day she might be tempted to act on her feelings.

Nick's car started. He drove away. She stepped back from the kitchen window and, closing her eyes, remembered how it had felt to have his face so very near to hers.

NICK HAD NEVER been so happy to be at work. Boring paperwork seemed like a breeze compared to changing diapers. And he'd rather put up with a lecture from the captain about results, results, results, than deal with a crying baby in the middle of the night.

The priority today, of course, was making progress on the Tara Lang case. There'd been no new developments overnight, which was probably a good thing. It meant that with any luck Tara remained alive and well.

Though he figured the teen was still in Hartford, Nick checked the crime reports from nearby centers just to be sure. He tensed when he read about a murder-rape, in Springfield, of a young woman about Tara's age, then felt a guilty wash of relief when he saw the victim had been already been identified as someone else. It seemed Tara had managed to survive another night out on the streets.

If, indeed, that was where she was.

"Hey, Gray, what's up?" Glenn Ferguson, his partner, sank into the chair next to Nick's. He was back in the city after tidying up loose ends on another assignment. "Any leads on the kid?"

"Just that tip yesterday."

"Right. The mall. You checked it out?"

"Yeah. Nothing. I didn't get even one positive ID."

"Too bad." Glenn leaned in for a look at the reports strewn over Nick's deck. Getting a whiff of Glenn's usual body odor, mixed with a good measure of stale alcohol and cigar smoke, Nick decided it was time to grab a refill of coffee.

Though he and Glenn had been partners for just a few weeks, Nick had already figured out that Glenn's idea of a good time involved an expensive smoke, one-too-many drinks at his favorite pub, and talking some woman into sharing his bed for the night.

Not that different from Nick's idea of a good time, perhaps, if you substituted a medium-rare steak for the cigar, but Nick was only thirty-four, while Glenn was pushing fifty.

Nick did not want to be in Glenn's shoes when he was fifty. But his failed marriage with Jessica wasn't a step in the right direction. They'd lasted less than a year as a married couple. It was a damn embarrassment. Worse was the potential impact on Mandy. His daughter would never have the security of living with a mother and a father under the same roof. How would that affect her?

As Nick reached for the full coffeepot, his thoughts shifted to Bridget. This morning her hair had been still damp from the shower and he'd been surprised at the way the baby-doll ringlets had framed her face.

He thought about how her house smelled and looked, so warm and inviting. Then about her eyes, that verdant green. Thinking about her gave him the same feeling as breathing in a lungful of cool, crisp air. More alive, yet somehow more relaxed, as well.

Nick filled a second cup, then returned to his desk. He handed a coffee to his partner, who gave him a grunt in return. Glenn shifted aside the report he'd been reading, exposing a family photograph taken for the Langs' Christmas cards.

The pose was casual. Vincent Lang was wearing a shirt and sweater, probably cashmere. His wife, wearing a silky blouse and pearls, stood behind him, one arm looped around his neck, her chin resting on his full head of silver hair. Just off to one side Tara posed stiffly. Her mother's hand rested lightly on her shoulder, but that was the only thing linking her to the attorney general and his wife.

"The kid doesn't look too happy," Glenn said. "I'm betting she didn't like having her photograph exploited for the sake of her father's political career."

Nick laughed. Glenn was on the money with that observation, no doubt about it. He studied the picture closer. "What about the wife? Do you think she minded?"

She had the expensively coiffed appearance of a woman who was used to the rich life. But did her eyes betray a little of the daughter's resentment? Or was he imagining that?

"Hard to say. Has anyone spoken with her?"

"I interviewed her late Wednesday afternoon." Nick pulled out his notebook. He'd gone to the Langs' house, an impressive Tudor home in the Hartford Golf Club neighborhood.

"Mrs. Lang was polite and cooperative, but also quite reserved. I asked her about Tuesday night and the alleged argument between Tara and her father."

"What did she say?"

Nick read from his notes: "Tara has always hated the obligations that come with her father's position. Those obligations are especially numerous at Christmas time. There are parties and other functions that Vincent simply must attend and many of them require his family's attendance, too."

Glenn snorted. "I'll just bet. So what did you say next?"

"I told her that I supposed most teenagers would resent having to attend a bunch of stuffy parties."

"I bet she didn't like that."

"You're right. Mrs. Lang looked offended then said, 'We're invited into some of the most beautiful homes in Hartford. Last night we had tickets to the gala performance of the *Nutcracker Ballet*.'"

"Big, frigging deal."

Nick nodded. Not too many fourteen-year-olds liked going to the ballet. But neither did they run away from home to escape the obligation. There was more going on in this kid's head than that.

And perhaps, in the mother's, too.

CHAPTER FIVE

LOOKING AFTER A six-month-old baby was hard work. A lot harder than looking after a dog. Scooping poop from a snowbank wasn't pleasant, but it beat changing diapers. And filling dog bowls wasn't nearly as fussy as spooning warm cereal into an easily distracted baby's mouth.

"Good thing you're so cute," Bridget said to Mandy as she tried again to get her to eat some of the cereal. But Mandy had uncanny timing, managing to push out her tongue at the exact moment Bridget brought the little spoon to her mouth.

Bridget laughed. "Maybe you're just not that hungry. Is that what you're trying to tell me?" She reached for the damp facecloth and cleaned Mandy's face. Mandy giggled, obviously finding this game very funny.

By the time she got Mandy down for her afternoon nap, Bridget realized she was going to earn every penny of the generous hourly rate that Nick was paying her.

She gazed at the sleeping baby, unable to resist touching the downy softness of her cheek. *You are so much work. But so worth it.*

She checked the monitor to make sure it was on, before going into the backyard to play with the dogs for a while. When they were tired, she went on the Internet to research diapers and baby-food recipes.

Baby food. A week ago she never would have guessed she'd be pureeing vegetables and wiping up baby spit. Mandy was adorable, but Bridget had to admit the real reason she'd agreed to the job was the girl's father.

She didn't know what it was about Nick that appealed to her. In real life, she didn't usually go for the playboy type. She liked dependable guys, with solid values and level heads. She'd had two serious relationships in her life. Two men she'd come very close to marrying.

They'd been wonderful men. Nothing like Nick. And yet…ever since he'd moved into the neighborhood she'd been fascinated by him.

She liked to think she saw hidden depths in the man. But maybe she was just kidding herself. Maybe, just maybe, she was as guilty of enjoying a charming, sexy man as the next woman.

Could it be? Was she, Bridget Humphrey, *human?*

Once Mandy woke up, Bridget went back into full-speed activity. First was Mandy's bottle, then another walk, which entailed bundling Mandy into the stroller and getting all four dogs on their leads and out the door.

It was later than usual when Bridget returned and soon the owners were coming to pick up their dogs. Foster left first. His owner, Diane House, was a teacher who dropped him off and picked him up on her walk to and from school.

As usual, Foster was waiting by the window and as soon as he spotted Diane, he ran to the front door and began running through his repertoire of tricks: sitting, holding out a paw, lying down, rolling over, then standing on his hind legs to dance.

Bridget opened the door, and Diane stuck her head inside, laughing at Foster's performance. "Good boy, Foster!"

She gave the little terrier his customary treat, then clipped him onto her leash. "Did you guys have a good day?"

"Sure did." Bridget explained about Mandy and how the dogs all seemed to enjoy having a baby around.

Before turning to leave, Diane sighed. "Just one more week, then school's out for the Christmas break. You remember Foster won't be back until January?"

Bridget nodded. All of her dogs would be staying home for several weeks over Christmas. It was good for them to have extra bonding time with their families. And it was good for her, too, giving her a chance to have a real holiday, as well.

Next to leave were Stanley and Herman. The wealthy couple who owned them had their nanny pick them up at the end of the day and she always arrived promptly at five.

Usually Lefty hated being the last to go home. The boxer would sit by the front door, desolate, waiting for his owner, Elizabeth, an executive who had no family and often worked late hours.

Today, though, he was distracted by Mandy and her endless fascination with his ears. Lefty gazed at her adoringly, letting her pull and stroke and pat to her heart's content. While they played, Bridget opened her mail. She loved this time of year, when she could look forward to receiving cards from friends and family rather than just the usual flyers and bills.

She was propping up that day's cards for display when the doorbell rang. Lefty snapped his head up and trotted to the front door. Elizabeth opened the unlocked door. "I've got him, Bridget. Thanks."

It took a moment for Mandy to register the fact that she'd been abandoned. She frowned, then stuck out her bottom lip. Bridget scooped her up before she could cry.

"You really do love those dogs, don't you, sweetie? How about I sing you some nursery rhymes?" Bridget soon found that Mandy responded best to old favorites—especially "Teensy, Weensy Spider."

As the time neared five-thirty, Bridget's thoughts turned to Nick. He should be here soon. She didn't like the way her pulse sped up just at the thought of seeing him again. This time when the doorbell rang, she checked her hair in the mirror. Earlier she'd combed it into a neat ponytail, but during her walk, the wind had wreaked havoc out of the wiry strands.

Ah well.

She opened the door with one hand, holding Mandy in the other. At first glance Nick seemed tired and discouraged, but as soon as he saw his daughter, his face relaxed into a genuine smile.

"How's my girl?" He held out his arms and Mandy went to him happily. "Was she cranky after getting so little sleep last night?"

Sexy guys looked even sexier holding a baby. Who would have guessed? "She was a doll, Nick. Come on in. She's ready to go. Just needs her snowsuit."

"Thanks, Bridget. I've got to tell you, it's a big relief for me, knowing that she's safe with you. Really lets me focus on the job."

"That's why you pay me the big bucks," she said lightly.

"After last night, I have no doubt you earn every cent. And more besides. I'll owe you big after this, Bridge. Anytime you need someone to walk your dogs, you'll know who to call."

She smiled, knowing his wasn't an empty offer. She led him through to the living room where Mandy's snowsuit was sitting on the stroller.

Bridget perched on a chair and watched as Nick expertly zipped up his daughter, then swirled her in the air, making her giggle with crazy abandon.

He was such a great guy. He really was. So why did he have so much trouble committing to relationships with women? She was dying to do his numbers and find out.

"Won't you please tell me your birth date?"

He made a face. "I thought we agreed to disagree on that numerology stuff."

"But aren't you even curious?" *She* certainly was. "You might be surprised at what your life path number has to tell you."

"I don't think so." He strapped his daughter into the stroller. Mandy clapped her hands together.

"By the way, I placed an order with Little Stork Diaper service today."

"Jessica left me with enough diapers for at least a month."

"She left you *disposable* diapers, Nick. Have you forgotten our deal?"

He gave her a sheepish smile. "No. But I was hoping you would."

"Using cloth rather than disposable reduces the waste in our landfills by about two tons per child."

"That's got to be an exaggeration."

She raised her eyebrows.

He sighed with apparent resignation. "Will I have to wash them?"

"No. Once a week, the diaper service picks up the soiled diapers and leaves us with more clean ones."

"We have to keep the dirty diapers for a week?" Nick looked disgusted by the prospect.

"In a special solution in a covered container. Don't worry. It shouldn't smell." She hoped.

"God, Bridget, I don't know. What if I promise to recycle absolutely everything I use for the rest of my life…after Mandy's out of diapers."

He gave her a smile so charming she almost caved. How could any woman say no to this man? But in all good conscience, she could not use disposable diapers when there were other more ecologically kind alternatives.

She was about to give him a lecture, when he backed down on his own.

"We had a deal. Yeah, I remember. I'll use the cloth diapers, Bridge. Is there anything else?"

"Organic, homemade, baby food," she reminded him brightly. "I made a batch of rice sweet potato and another of barley carrot this afternoon after our walk. I froze them in ice-cube containers. You can feed Mandy one for dinner tonight."

"Rice sweet potato, huh?"

"She'll love it. Just thaw it in the microwave, then serve." She removed the plastic bag from her freezer and stowed it in the diaper bag.

"Sounds simple enough, even for me." He had started to wheel the stroller down the hall when he suddenly noticed her display of Christmas cards.

"What the hell." He picked up one of the cards, frowned, then glanced at her. "Where did you get this?"

She took the card from his hand, slightly annoyed by his tone. "In the mail. Why?"

"You know Attorney General Lang?"

"His wife is a client of mine."

Nick let out a low whistle. "Interesting."

"Why is this such a big deal? Do *you* know the Lang family?"

"Unfortunately, yes." He removed a photograph from his shirt pocket and showed it to her.

Annabel's daughter stared up at her.

Why did Nick have a picture of Tara? Before she could ask the question, she knew the answer. "Tara is the runaway you're looking for."

CHAPTER SIX

"THAT'S RIGHT," Nick said, his expression serious.

"Annabel didn't tell me." Bridget had guessed something was wrong, but she hadn't realized it was this serious. Oh, God. Poor Annabel.

"You've talked to Annabel recently?" Nick asked.

"She was here last night, wanting me to do an analysis for her daughter. She admitted that she was worried about Tara. But she didn't tell me she'd run away from home."

Bridget studied the photograph again. This close-up provided a much clearer portrayal of Tara than the family picture on the Christmas card. Tara was at that awkward adolescent stage, not yet pretty, but with potential. While the picture wasn't flattering, it had captured a lot of emotion.

Hostility for one. Dig a little deeper, Bridget thought, and you'd find loneliness. Behind that, hurt.

This was not a street-smart girl. Bridget could almost see the vulnerability oozing from her pores. "Were there any positive developments in the search today?"

Nick's sigh was heavy. "We're working on a

number of leads. Her father seems pretty certain she's hiding out at a friend's house, but after today, we're not so sure. Unless she has a friend her parents don't know about. If so, we're hoping she was in e-mail contact with the person. Our technical guys are having a crack at the hard drive from Tara's computer as we speak."

"You think she could have met someone online?"

"It's one of the possibilities we're pursuing. I'd like to follow up on it tomorrow."

"Tomorrow is Saturday."

"Yeah. I was meaning to ask you about that. I know, it's a hell of a favor, but could you possibly watch Mandy for a few hours?"

For Annabel's sake and Tara's, she wanted to say yes. At the same time she worried that Nick would get into the habit of passing off his responsibilities as a father. "I have plans in the morning. Besides that, even though your work is important, your daughter needs you, too."

"If you think I'm looking for excuses to avoid Mandy, you're wrong."

"No. I didn't mean—"

"Time is of the essence in a case like this. The longer Tara is out on the street the greater the chance that we don't find her. Or that we find her too late."

Bridget swallowed at his grim reminder. She studied the photograph once again before passing it back to him. She couldn't imagine the agony Annabel must be going through right now. Why had she been so secretive last night? In the past Annabel had shared many details about her life and her marriage, the sort of information you'd only tell someone you trusted implicitly.

"I wish Annabel had told me this. I still can't understand why she didn't."

"I'd guess her husband had something to do with that. Vincent Lang has made a big deal about keeping this secret."

"But why?"

"He claims to be worried that if news gets out that his daughter is on the street, she could become a kidnapping target. There's more than one unscrupulous ex-con with a vendetta against our esteemed attorney general."

"But if the family went to the media with her disappearance surely you'd have a better chance of getting a tip from the public?"

Nick said nothing.

"Only Vincent Lang doesn't want the public to know," Bridget said slowly, figuring out the attorney general's motives as she spoke.

"Exactly. Lang has a reputation as a devoted family man. Remember those campaign ads that show him coaching his daughter's softball team?"

She did.

"Voters would have a hard time buying that image if they knew his daughter had run away from home."

It was a cynical view, but Annabel had told Bridget enough about her husband that Nick's assessment rang true. Still… "Could he really be so ambitious that he'd put his career ahead of his daughter's safety?"

Nick brushed a finger over Mandy's cheek. "Hard to believe, isn't it?"

Bridget felt sick to her stomach. How could Annabel go along with Vincent's games when her own daughter's life was at stake? That part *didn't* ring true. Annabel loved her daughter deeply. Of that Bridget had no doubt.

"You're right, Nick. You need to work the case. I'll be glad to watch Mandy for a while tomorrow."

"Just an hour or two would help."

"I can think of something else that might help." She eyed him assessingly, wondering if he'd be open to what she had to say. "The reason Annabel came to see me last night was to get a reading for her daughter. I didn't understand the significance then, but now I realize that I may have uncovered something important. It isn't confidential. It's information any numerologist would glean just from knowing Tara's birth date."

Nick's expression turned carefully polite. "Um, thanks, Bridget, but maybe we should talk about that another time. Mandy must be overheating in her snowsuit by now."

Mandy looked fine. She was playing with the drawstrings on her hood.

"If you'd just hear me out. You never know—"

"I appreciate that you want to help. But we'll find Tara the regular way—with careful, methodical police procedures. It's the best way, Bridge. Trust me on this."

DAMN, BUT HE WISHED Bridget would stop peddling her numerology crap at him. She seemed so smart and together most of the time.

He thought of the way she'd winced when he'd refused her offer. Maybe he'd been a little too harsh. She was a great person in so many ways and he owed her. He supposed he could have been polite and listened to what she had to say. But between work and Mandy, he didn't have a lot of spare time right now.

It hadn't been snowing when Nick had arrived at Bridget's, but now snowflakes were falling, heavy with moisture, landing with silent splats on sidewalks that had just been shoveled clean from the last dump. Nick wheeled the stroller briskly toward his house.

One point Bridget had made had struck home…he couldn't let work consume him to the point that he neglected Mandy. Other single parents juggled work and parenthood. Surely he could, too.

As soon as he was home, though, and had Mandy out of her snowsuit, she started to cry. He held her close, feeling helpless.

Was she upset because they hadn't gone for a longer walk? It was almost six. So maybe she was hungry?

Working with his free hand, he microwaved one of the food cubes Bridget had given him. He checked to make sure it wasn't too hot, then tried feeding Mandy. He managed to get some of the organic goop down her throat, but most of it ended up in her hair and all over her face and hands.

God, what a mess.

Bath was next, and he expected to see Mandy's

usual big smiles when he placed her in the small tub of warm water, but clearly Mandy was in no mood to enjoy *anything* right now.

She cried as he gave her the quickest bath on record. "Sorry, honey, but we've got to do this." He didn't get her super clean, but at least the chunks of food were no longer in her hair.

He dried her, then strapped on a fresh diaper for the night, trying not to imagine how much harder this was going to be when he had to start dealing with old-fashioned cloth diapers. From an ecological viewpoint, he knew Bridget was right. But practically speaking...he wasn't so sure.

Finally Mandy was clean—well, mostly clean— dressed, and ready for her bedtime bottle. All her crying had given her the hiccups and as she gulped down the milk, tears were still leaking from her eyes.

Nick felt a little like crying himself.

"I'm sorry your dad's such a klutz." He kissed the top of her head, feeling his heart surge with a warm, protective feeling that was familiar yet seemed to grow stronger with each hour he spent with his baby girl.

He remembered something Gavin had said to him after Mandy's birth. *Welcome to fatherhood, bro. Your life will never be the same.*

Man, it was so true.

Holding Mandy close to his heart as she drank from her bottle, he thought about the missing teenager and tried to imagine how her parents must be feeling right now.

If it was him, he'd be going crazy.

He wondered what Tara Lang had had for dinner tonight. Where was she planning to sleep for the night? Was she really hiding out in a friend's basement, as her father thought? Or was this going to be her third night on the street?

Nick thought over all he'd done, trying to see if he'd missed anything. Interviews with Tara's friends and teachers had led nowhere. All her favorite haunts were being watched closely. So far, except for that one tip about the mall, she hadn't been spotted anywhere.

Now they had her computer to work with. He sure hoped the techies were able to find something worthwhile. But somehow Nick couldn't muster much optimism about that. He was bothered by the parents, the feeling he had that they weren't being completely open with the police. He wished he knew what they were hiding.

Family secrets that didn't matter to anyone but them? Or relevant information that would help in the search for Tara?

Mandy had finished her bottle and her eyelids were fluttering closed as he bent to settle her into the crib. As soon as her body hit the sheets, though, her eyes popped back open. She took one look at him, then started sobbing again.

"Oh, Mandy, honey, what's the matter?" He picked her up and held her close. Immediately she grew quiet. He tried to relax in his armchair, but she started crying again, and wouldn't stop.

For an hour, it went like that, until he caved and retrieved her snowsuit. As soon as he started bundling her up, Mandy stopped crying. Ten minutes into their midnight stroll, she was asleep.

He crept inside without turning on any lights other than the one over the stove and the night-light in the hall. Should he let Mandy sleep in the stroller again? But remembering how she'd woken in the middle of the night yesterday, he decided to try and transfer her into the crib where she'd be more comfortable.

It didn't work. Nick felt like pulling out his hair as his daughter started crying again. It seemed he had two choices. Walk with her outside in the stroller, or pace around his home with her in his arms.

So Nick held her.

And walked.

And with every circuit he made of the living room, his thoughts circled back to Bridget. He couldn't understand why.

He'd known her for five years, yet he knew very little about her background or other interests beyond the dogs and numerology.

She'd said she had plans for Saturday. He wondered what they were. Maybe she had a boy-friend. Surprisingly, he didn't like the thought of that. But she probably did.

He could imagine some men finding her very attractive. Not him, necessarily, although she did have a certain girl-next-door appeal. Like that actress who'd played…oh, hell, he couldn't remember the name of actress or the movie. The point was, the woman had been pretty in a quiet sort of way, and sexy without even trying.

Like Bridget.

Finally, at quarter to midnight, a miracle occurred. Nick gently lowered Mandy into her crib and she didn't wake up. He watched for a few seconds, holding his breath, then slowly backed out of the room.

He still hadn't had any dinner himself, hadn't watched the news or the *Jon Stewart* show, or checked his e-mail. In short, none of the stuff that usually filled his evenings after work.

But he was so tired, he didn't care.

Still dressed in the shirt and pants he'd worn to work, Nick crawled into bed.

ON SATURDAY MORNING Bridget picked out a Christmas tree with her ex-boyfriend Troy Whitman. Troy loaded the tree onto the top of his Volvo station wagon, then helped her bring it inside and position it in the tree stand.

"Still crooked." Bridget was standing back to get a view from the kitchen. After Troy shifted the tree over a few inches, she moved to a different vantage point in the living room. "Now it's too far the other way."

She couldn't see Troy's expression—his head was lost amidst the pine branches—but she heard him curse. "Good Lord, woman, make up your mind, would you?"

"That's perfect. Hold it right there." She hurried to tighten the screws on the stand while he held the tree in place.

Finally the job was done to her satisfaction. The two of them stood back to admire the final result.

"A little spindly, wouldn't you say?" was Troy's assessment.

"If I wanted perfection, I'd go with artificial." They had the same argument every year. She went to the kitchen to pour traditional eggnogs. They clinked glasses.

"To you, Troy. Congratulations on becoming a daddy."

He beamed. "You should try it, Bridget. Marriage. Parenthood. It's all pretty great."

"One day I will," she said, but she wondered when that day would come. Troy made a wonderful husband and father, yet when she'd had the chance to marry him, she'd backed away.

Her parents had been so disappointed. When her mother asked her why, all she'd been able to say was, *It doesn't feel right.*

"*What* doesn't feel right?" her mother had asked.

Bridget had no answer to that. She still didn't. All she knew was that friendship was all she wanted from Troy. She linked her arm with his as they polished off the eggnog. "I'm so glad Deirdre doesn't mind you helping me with my tree."

She and Troy had started the tradition when they were both students at Harvard. Over the years, even after their amiable breakup, they'd remained friends and continued with the tree routine. Bridget had wondered if Troy's marriage might mark the end of it. So far it hadn't.

"According to Deirdre, there are certain jobs you should never do with your spouse, like hanging wallpaper. Putting up Christmas trees is another of them."

"So who helps Deirdre with your tree?"

"Her dad."

"Hmm. Could you see *my* dad helping me with my tree?"

"Yeah, right. Your father doesn't put up his own tree. Why would he help you with yours?"

They both laughed. Troy knew her intellectual parents well. Her father and mother were absolutely hopeless around the house. They didn't even own a hammer or a screwdriver.

Troy's family was also intellectual—and rich, besides. It was a world Bridget couldn't imagine fitting into. But Troy, with his beautiful wife and career in high finance, managed to move in almost any social circle with ease. She didn't hold this against him. Troy didn't have a snobbish bone in his body.

"Mom and Dad have never even seen my home. When they heard I was starting a doggy day care, it was the final straw for them. And you know how they felt about the numerology."

"Maybe you should bite the bullet and invite them over this Christmas. Eventually they're going to accept that they can't change you so they might as well accept you as you are."

"Do you really think that's possible?"

"No." He laughed. "But you should still invite them over."

When his drink was finished, Troy rinsed his glass and left it in the sink. "I should get back. Deirdre wants to go shopping this afternoon while Jeffery is napping."

Bridget walked him to the front door and, as he was leaving, passed him a bag filled with gifts for the family. "Have a wonderful Christmas, Troy. And thanks so much."

He wrapped an arm around her waist and gave her an affectionate squeeze. A few yards away, Bridget heard a man clear his throat. She looked past Troy to the gate.

Nick stood in the snow with the stroller. "Sorry. Am I interrupting?"

CHAPTER SEVEN

NICK HAD CONSIDERED the possibility that Bridget might have a boyfriend. But he'd never pictured someone like this guy. Bridget was New Age bohemian. This guy was pure establishment. Tall, blond, a sharp dresser. His jeans looked pressed and he had a dapper wool scarf and polished black boots. Who looked that good on a weekend?

Who looked that good, ever?

"Nick, I'd like you to meet my friend, Troy Whitman. Troy, this is one of my clients, Nick Gray, and his daughter, Mandy."

"Bridget babysits my daughter," Nick said, wanting to make it clear he wasn't one of her numerology clients.

He'd never taken an instant dislike to someone who wasn't a criminal before—which this clean-cut guy clearly wasn't—and his strong apathy toward the other man caught him off guard.

He made an effort to smile as he shook Troy's hand.

"Bridget and I go way back," Troy said, his tone friendly. "To our Harvard days."

"Harvard?" Nick looked from him to Bridget. *Harvard?*

"Well, I'd better get moving. It was nice to meet you. And your daughter's adorable." He began to leave. Then stopped. "Bridget, I almost forgot. Deirdre asked me to remind you about our open house on New Year's Day."

Bridget nodded and said something in reply. Nick didn't pay much attention. He was processing Troy's words and the obvious fact that he was with this woman named Deirdre, which meant that he and Bridget really were just friends.

This deduction was confirmed when he saw Troy get into a Volvo with an infant car seat strapped into the back. Not only was the guy married. He had a kid, too.

"Coming inside?" Bridget asked, holding the door open wide to make room for the stroller. Once they were in, she undid the straps that held Mandy tight, and lifted her out.

"Hello, sweetie."

As Bridget peeled off Mandy's snowsuit, Nick ran his gaze over her place. Barely realizing that he'd slipped into investigator mode, he noticed two dirty glasses in the sink, a bedraggled Christmas tree in the corner of the living room. But his mind kept coming back to one fact.

"I never pictured you as the Harvard type."

"I wasn't," she agreed, not adding any more detail than that.

"So you and Troy are old friends, huh?" He shoved the stroller out of the way, into a corner.

"That's right." Mandy reached out for a set of plastic measuring cups on the counter. Bridget settled her on the fluffy white carpet, then gave her the cups to play with.

"Just friends?" Troy clearly wasn't a romantic fling. Nick didn't know why he couldn't let it go.

"Now we are. He's married."

His mind latched on to the word *now*. "So you used to date him?"

"A long time ago." She sighed, exasperated. "What's with all the questions?"

He wished he knew. "I don't know. There was something about the guy that bothered me." *Like the fact that he'd had his arms around Bridget.*

Hell, that's what this was, Nick realized, shocked. Jealousy. But why? He wasn't involved with Bridget. Not *that* way. He wasn't even interested.

"What did you study at Harvard?" He wasn't surprised she'd gone to university. But Harvard?

"Physics."

"Did you get your degree?"

She hesitated, then nodded.

"What about Whitman? Did he study physics, too?"

"No. Finance. Look, Nick, I'm flattered that you find my past so fascinating, but shouldn't we be focusing on Tara right now? That is why you wanted me to watch Mandy, right?"

He struggled to switch gears in his head. When he latched onto a puzzle, it was almost impossible for him to let it go. Right now he was wondering who Bridget Humphrey really was. In the face of contradictory evidence, he couldn't decide.

"By the way, I called Annabel last night. No answer. So I went over the notes I'd made the previous night," Bridget said. She stepped beside him, close enough that he caught a whiff of sweet, light perfume. "Tara is naturally secretive and isolated. She feels like a misfit, Nick, which would be exaggerated by her age and the pressures of being a teenager. On top of all that, she's sensitive, with a tendency to be somewhat naive."

Despite Bridget's confident delivery, he wasn't impressed. "Doesn't sound that unusual for a fourteen-year-old girl."

"Know a lot of fourteen-year-old girls, do you? I would argue she *is* different. And she knows it. Tara is more vulnerable than most girls her age. My guess is that she would have difficulty fitting in at school."

"According to her parents, she has lots of friends."

Bridget shook her head. "Despite what her mother and father choose to believe, I'd guess she doesn't. The friends that she *does* have probably aren't very close."

She seemed so sure about this, he was almost convinced. Then he reminded himself what the basis of her opinion was. Tara's birth date.

"That's interesting, but I really need to—"

She put a hand on his arm. "Just let me finish. It seems unlikely to me that Tara would be hiding at a friend's house. I see her with someone older. Someone she trusts. Unfortunately, Tara's naiveté may have led her to trust the wrong person."

Despite his skepticism, Nick felt a shiver start between his shoulders and run down his back.

"This girl has no defenses, Nick. You have to find her."

NICK HAD NO REASON to believe that Bridget's analysis was anything other than an educated guess. Only one thing made his stomach tighten in a painful knot as he settled into his desk with an extralarge cup of take-out coffee in hand.

His own instincts were telling him the exact same thing that Bridget's numerology charts were telling her.

This kid was in trouble. Even if her parents—in particular, her father—didn't want to believe it.

Vincent Lang was convinced that his daughter was hiding out with a friend, maliciously causing her parents to worry because of a misguided adolescent sense of entitlement.

But which friend? He and Glenn had conducted dozens of interviews at Tara's exclusive private school. He skimmed through the reports again, then went back to read them more carefully.

His feeling of unease grew.

Reading between the lines of Tara's schoolmates, he saw the truth of what Bridget had said about Tara being a misfit. These kids her parents thought were her friends didn't *know* her. They weren't Tara's friends.

"Yeah, I knew Tara," one of them had said. "We hung out sometimes when our parents were visiting one another." In other words, when she felt *obliged* to.

Another classmate mentioned that Tara usually ate her lunch alone, listening to her iPod.

Nick's vision blurred. He rubbed his eyes then took a swig of black coffee. God, his neck and shoulders were tight.

"Bored?" A colleague sitting in front of a computer a few yards away was also stretching. They were the only two in the room right now.

"Nah." He rotated his neck from one side to the other. "Just not getting much sleep. I have a six-month-old daughter."

"Say no more." The guy gave him a sympathetic smile. "My wife and I had twins three years ago."

"Twins?" He couldn't imagine how hard *two* babies must be.

"They didn't sleep through the night until they were a year old."

Oh, God. A full year of sleep deprivation? Nick didn't know how anyone could survive that. Last night Mandy had woken at two, then again at five. Jessica's schedule made no mention of these nocturnal wakings. Next time his ex called, he'd have to ask her what was up, though he suspected he knew.

Mandy was missing her mother and her usual schedule. It would take time for her to realize she was safe with her dad, too.

He clamped down on a familiar wave of guilt. He hated the fact that his daughter was starting life in less than ideal circumstances, being shuttled back and forth between mother and father. Wherever she went she was loved, which was good, but he wished that she could have had more.

Stability. Security. A mother and father who loved each other as well as her.

He'd had all that, at least for the first nine years of his life. Even having his father die so young hadn't been as traumatic as it could have been, thanks to his older brothers.

Nick took another drink of coffee, then turned to the report from the computer experts.

They'd pulled off a lot of information from Tara's computer. She had thousands of downloaded songs and used MSN Messenger occasionally. But most of her time at the computer seemed to be spent on Facebook. She had a page listed there, using the name LikeJoni.

He soon realized this was an homage to Joni Mitchell. Interesting that this kid would choose a hero whose height of popularity was decades before Tara was even born. Maybe this was another indication that she didn't feel connected to her own generation.

One thing was clear from Tara's Facebook page. Songwriting was her passion. She had a list of her favorite songs as well as some lyrics of her own.

Nick read through them, and while they were full of teenaged angst, he saw nothing especially violent or self-destructive.

Still, the site had a lonely, almost desperate edge to it. He thought about Bridget's analysis. So far, he had to admit, she'd been spot-on.

As he read more about the girl, Nick realized that conspicuously absent was any mention of softball. Did she enjoy the sport? Or was her participation just one more thing she did to please her parents?

He made a note to consult the gym teacher at Tara's school, then went back to review the details of her Facebook page. Facebook allowed users to identify "friends" or people who were allowed access to the information, pictures and such, on their Web page.

He didn't recognize any of Tara's friends from the list her parents had given him. These seemed to be kids who shared her passion for songwriting, from various locations across North America. Checking out this list would take a long time, probably with futile results.

Nick went back to Tara's MSN account. He reviewed her list of friends here, too, looking for signs that she may have struck up a dangerous relationship with someone online.

Nothing had been red-flagged by the computer guys. He couldn't spot any obvious problems, either.

Nick leaned back in his chair and finished off his coffee, waiting for the caffeine to kick in. He had more work to do, but all he wanted was to go home and find out what Mandy and Bridget were up to. He'd taken his daughter for a long walk this morning. At one point he'd scooped up some snow, formed it into a ball, then placed it in Mandy's hands.

Her big eyes had grown perfectly round with wonder when the ball disintegrated at her touch. He smiled at the memory. Now he understood what people meant when they talked about seeing the world from a child's eyes.

He couldn't wait to see more of it.

WHEN BRIDGET OPENED the door to him, Nick was greeted with the sound of Christmas carols playing in the background. *You better be good, I'm telling you why…*

She smiled in welcome, then turned serious. "Did you find anything helpful from Tara's computer?"

"A few leads…but nothing very promising."

"You look exhausted. Come in for a minute. I just took a batch of cookies out of the oven."

Stepping into her home was like entering a different world, certainly much different from the police headquarters he had just left, but different from his place, too, and those of the people he usually hung out with. He felt enveloped with warmth and good smells—baking cookies mingled with the fresh aroma of pine. Mandy sat on the floor a few feet from the Christmas tree. She was staring at it, mesmerized.

Bridget had decorated while he was at work. Colored lights glowed from all the branches. Garlands of sparkly tinsel, colored bells and myriads of paper angels made it one of the most garish trees he had ever seen.

"Isn't it beautiful?" Bridget came into the room holding a tray with two steaming mugs and a plate of cookies, which she set on the coffee table.

"Um…no comment on the tree."

"Don't be a Scrooge, Nick. Mandy loves it."

He couldn't deny the truth of that. The electric lights were reflected in Mandy's big blue eyes as she stared at it. He felt like snapping his fingers in front of her face to break the trance.

Instead, he settled on the floor next to his daughter. She seemed happy that he was here, but also in no hurry to go anywhere.

Bridget sat on the floor, too, and passed him one of the mugs. The hot chocolate was incredible. Not the packaged kind, but made from real milk, real cocoa.

"Your daughter loved watching me decorate. She was so gentle when I let her touch the paper angels."

She placed a small container of puffed wheat cereal in front of Mandy, who carefully selected one grain of the puffed cereal and awkwardly placed it into her mouth.

"Next year you can have a cookie, too," Bridget promised as she bit into one herself. Noticing him watching her, she raised her eyebrows. "Want one? Go ahead."

She held out the plate to him, but he shook his head, replacing the mug of cocoa rather than taking another sip. There was something almost too perfect about this scene, and he found himself resisting both the refreshments and the mood.

"You're one of those people who really get into the holiday spirit, aren't you?" he asked.

"Of course. It's fun. What about you?"

He shook his head. "I usually work so the guys with families can spend the day with their kids."

"This year you're one of those guys," Bridget said gently. "Have you thought about how you and Mandy will celebrate Christmas?"

"Mandy's so young. I don't think it needs to be a big deal. We'll probably get invited to my brother Matt's for dinner."

"I saw a photograph of your brothers at your place. Is Matt the one with glasses?"

"Yeah. And the tallest one is our middle brother, Gavin. He and his wife, Allison, live in New Hampshire with their kids. They'll probably drive up for the holidays."

"What about Matt? Is he married?"

"Yup. He and his second wife, Jane, are both lawyers. Matt has a thirteen-year-old son and a four-year-old daughter from his first marriage. They'll be there, as well as my mom."

"Sounds like a big family. How many kids does Gavin have?"

"He had twin girls, but..." Nick stopped. The accident was still hard to talk about. "Tory turned eight this fall, but three years ago her sister, Samantha, was struck by a motorcycle when she was running across the street."

"Oh, Nick."

"It was a horrible time for the family. My brother pulled his life together, though. He moved with Tory to Squam Lake so they could have a fresh start. He had some issues to sort through with the mother of his twins, but once that was taken care of, he fell in love with his next-door neighbor. Now that he and Allison have a new baby, I don't think they could be happier."

"I'm glad the family was able to heal after such a terrible tragedy."

Nick nodded. He still thought of his niece often. Samantha had been a real card, truly one of a kind. Whenever he heard of an accident involving a youngster at work, the old pain would sneak up on him. He couldn't imagine how much harder it must be for Gavin and Tory.

"Our family's been through a lot. Everyone thought after Matt and Jane were married that life would settle down. Then Jessica left me and all hell broke out again. My mother still hasn't forgiven me." He managed a grin, though there was little amusing about his mother's disapproval.

"Why does your mom blame you?"

"Isn't it obvious? I don't have a reputation for long-term relationships, Bridget."

"I thought you said Jessica walked out on the marriage?"

"She said I married her because of the baby. That I didn't really love her. And you know—it was true." He shrugged. More pretense on his part, he knew. Acting as though it hadn't mattered that much.

But if that were true, why did his gut burn every time he thought of his failed marriage? True, he hadn't loved Jessica when he'd proposed. But he'd tried to love her. He'd thought, over time, it might happen.

"I'm sorry the marriage didn't work out the way you hoped."

Bridget's green eyes were luminous. She wasn't tearing up, was she? "It's water under the bridge. Next time I won't be so stupid."

"Wanting to marry the mother of your child doesn't seem stupid to me."

CHAPTER EIGHT

"Maybe not for most men. But if Jessica hadn't left when she did, I probably would have bailed, eventually."

Bridget gave him a crooked smile. "You persist in thinking the worst of yourself, don't you?"

"I'm a realist." Or he tried to be. Getting married had been a leap of faith, and though he had a hard time admitting it, he really had tried to make Jessica happy.

Gavin said having a baby put a strain on any marriage, let alone a brand-new one, but Nick suspected he'd said that only to alleviate Nick's guilt.

At any rate, he had gained one thing from the experience. His daughter.

He'd failed as a husband. No way was he going to fail as a father.

"Thanks again for watching Mandy this afternoon."

"It was no problem. I'm just sorry you didn't have more luck with Tara's computer."

Worried that Bridget was about to bring up numerology again, Nick grabbed Mandy's snowsuit. "We'd better get going. Mandy, ready to go home?"

Usually nothing made his daughter happier than the prospect of a walk, but today, for some reason, she protested as he zipped her into her warm clothing.

By the time he'd strapped her into the stroller, she was crying. Bridget looked concerned. "Maybe she's hungry. Do you want me to heat some dinner for her?"

Tempting offer. But he was the dad. He couldn't keep pawning the care of his daughter off on Bridget. "I'll feed her as soon as I get home."

"Okay." But as she stood at the door, watching them off, he could see the worry lines still on her face.

Frankly, he didn't blame her.

ONCE SHE WAS ALONE, Bridget started the movie she always watched on the day she put up her tree. But though she stared at the screen, her thoughts lingered on Nick. The longer she knew him, the more he puzzled her. He liked to pretend that his failed marriage hadn't fazed him, but she could tell that the divorce had left deep wounds.

He was so hard on himself. Did that come from being the youngest of three brothers? Being an only child herself, she didn't know what that would have been like. Clearly Matthew and Gavin were both successful in their careers and families. Maybe Nick found it hard to live up to their example.

But he wasn't doing that badly. He'd just been promoted at work. And he was trying hard with Mandy. He really was.

Or was she simply making excuses for him, because she found him the sexiest man she'd ever met? This silly crush of hers wasn't going anywhere. Why couldn't she get over it?

Nick was not her kind of guy. She loved movies like *It's A Wonderful Life. Die Hard* and *Harder* and *Hardest* would be more his style.

He liked women in high heels. She wore clogs. He liked fishnet stockings. She wore wool socks. If Nick Gray, rather than George Bailey, had inherited the Savings and Loan, he would have sold it and moved to New York City and spent the money on wine, women and song.

And yet, on those long walks they'd had with the dogs, they'd had no trouble finding lots to talk about. Maybe they weren't quite as different as they appeared.

Oh, stop thinking, Bridget. Watch the movie.

She tried to focus on the story she loved so much, but her mind kept wandering and so she turned the TV off. How was Nick making out now? Had Mandy stopped crying? If she hadn't—could Nick cope? He looked exhausted and she knew he wasn't getting much sleep at night.

Should she give him a call?

Or let him struggle on his own?

MANDY CRIED ALL THE WAY HOME. As Nick pushed the snowy stroller through his front door he was greeted by cold, dark and silence. Quite a contrast to the home he'd just left.

He contemplated the chores in front of him. Remove Mandy's snowsuit, heat up her dinner, somehow get her to eat most of it, give her a bath, change her diaper…

Just thinking about all that was exhausting.

He wanted a beer and pizza. He wanted to watch the game tonight. To take a nap.

All regular activities in his former life.

But based on his recent experience with Mandy, he wouldn't have time for any of that. Right now he'd settle for calming Mandy down and getting her to smile at him.

He released her from the stroller and pulled off the warm snowsuit. Her face was red and damp. Maybe she'd been crying because she was too hot? Although it was snowing again, the temperature outside was moderate.

But even once he had her snowsuit off, Mandy kept crying.

He tucked her close to his chest as he made his way to the kitchen.

And still she cried.

He warmed a frozen cube of the organic baby food. When she wouldn't eat a bite of it, he tried a bottle. She turned her head away and howled even louder.

"Honey, I'm sorry. I wouldn't eat this stuff, either. But you're too young for pizza or beer."

Was her new cloth diaper wet? He checked. It was dry.

"Please, Mandy, please. I know you can't talk. But can you give me some kind of sign?" He was getting desperate. Holding his daughter to his heart, he resumed pacing.

What was he doing wrong? Why did she always

seem so happy at Bridget's and so miserable here with him?

He clenched his jaw and kept on pacing. Maybe a walk in the stroller? But he'd had her in the stroller, earlier, and that hadn't solved a thing.

Nick was desperately trying to think of a second option when his phone rang. It was Bridget. As soon as she heard Mandy crying, she asked him if he wanted to come over.

"Yes. Thank you. Yes."

WHEN BRIDGET OPENED the door, Nick felt a huge release in tension. "I've never been so glad to see someone in my life. I don't know what I'm doing wrong."

Hearing Bridget's voice, Mandy calmed down. She clung to her for a moment, then had the nerve to reach for her dad.

"I'm glad I'm no longer chopped liver," Nick said, taking back his daughter. "But what the hell is going on here? At home she wouldn't stop crying no matter what I did. I tried feeding her, giving her a bottle, distracting her with songs and toys…"

Exhaustion washed over him. "I figured the problem had to be me. But look at her now." She was cuddling into him like a newborn kitten, as if there was no other place she'd rather be. "Why wouldn't she do this earlier?"

"I'm not sure. At six months she's definitely old enough to be sensitive to her surroundings. Maybe my house is more like her mother's?"

"My place is kind of stark." Why hadn't he taken the time to fix it up? He would have, if he'd realized it would matter to Mandy.

"But that's just a guess on my part. Mandy's entitled to be a little confused since her normal routine has changed so much."

He nodded, feeling the familiar sting of guilt that his daughter didn't have the benefit of living in a stable, two-parent home.

"If she wouldn't eat at your place, she's probably starving by now."

Bridget warmed up some food, then left Nick to do the feeding while she ran a bath for the baby. Within thirty minutes, they had Mandy ready for bed. Pooped from all her crying, she fell asleep the instant she was placed in the portable crib in Bridget's spare room.

"Poor thing wore herself out." Nick gazed at his daughter feeling both love and worry. Taking care of her needs seemed so easy when he was working as part of a team. How did single parents manage on their own?

"You look exhausted, too," Bridget said frankly.

"I haven't slept more than three hours straight since Mandy moved in," he admitted. "I hate to say it, but being a single dad is harder than working nights."

Bridget gestured to the bed. "Feel free to crash for the night, if you want."

Nick eyed the bed longingly. But besides being tired, he was also starving. He hadn't eaten a decent meal since Mandy had moved in, either. "Have you had dinner?"

"I was about to order some sushi and watch a movie on DVD."

"How about I treat you to the sushi?" Nick pulled out his cell phone. "I have the local sushi bar on speed dial—that is, if you don't mind some company?"

"Not if you're up to watching *It's a Wonderful Life* with Jimmy Stewart."

"Bring it on."

"There aren't any exploding buildings, car chases or grisly murders."

"I know what I'm in for," he assured her. Once he'd finished placing the food order, Bridget hit the play button on the remote control.

Nick settled on the sofa a few feet from her. This was nice, he told himself. Fun and casual. It was a novelty to be spending a Saturday night with a woman who wasn't his date. It was probably good for him to have a platonic relationship like this.

Bridget stretched out her feet to a nearby footstool. Her top rose an inch at the maneuver and his attention was drawn to her flat midriff, then the flaring of her hips.

She definitely did hide a nice set of curves under her bohemian outfits.

Not that it made any difference to him. Being a guy, it was only natural that he noticed, that was all.

Thirty minutes into the movie the doorbell rang and Nick got up to pay the bill. He opened the containers on the kitchen counter, then made up two plates and brought them to the living room.

"Thanks, Nick." Bridget's attention hardly wavered

from the screen as she ate her meal. He found her absorption in the old movie cute.

When they reached the part of the story when the uncle accidentally mislays the day's deposit, Nick hooted. "This is my favorite part."

"You've seen this before?"

"Sure. My mom loved old movies. She used to make me and my brothers watch one with her every Sunday night. *To Kill a Mockingbird* was Matt's favorite. Gavin liked *Casablanca*."

"Is Matt a romantic?"

"He's all about honor and doing the right thing. Actually, both my brothers are. Want another crab roll?"

"No, thanks. What about you, Nick? What are you all about?"

"Good food, Bridge." He winked at her. "And classic movies. That's what I'm into." He polished off the crab roll, then continued eating until all the food was gone.

He patted his full belly then relaxed his arm across the back of the sofa, inadvertently touching a stray curl of her hair.

She'd been wearing a ponytail earlier, but had pulled it out so she could lean her head against the back of the sofa. Now her hair flowed in waves down to her shoulders. He tugged gently on the strand next to his fingers.

She looked at him, puzzled.

"So you and Troy. How long did you go out?" Now why had he asked that? He hadn't even been aware of thinking about Troy.

"A few years."

"Years? You must have really been serious. Why didn't you get married?"

"Funny. That's what my parents wanted to know, too. But we were young and…I don't know. I think we made better friends than…"

"Lovers?"

She swallowed, then nodded.

"No fireworks, huh? What about your next boyfriend?"

"Who said there was another one?"

"Just a guess…am I right?"

She nodded. "I had one other serious relationship after Troy."

"And what was wrong that time?"

"Nothing really." She shrugged. "He was a great guy, too. Sometimes I wonder if I should have stuck it out and done the marriage thing."

"Well, I'm no expert, but if these relationships were as lackluster as they sound, then I think you made the right call. My only question is why you hung around as long as you did. If the sex appeal isn't there from the beginning, it sure isn't going to come later."

"Who said there wasn't any sex appeal?"

Nick laughed. Who was she trying to kid? "Let me save you some time with your next boyfriend. If your world doesn't rock the first time he kisses you, then move on."

"The first kiss, huh? It's that important?"

"Definitely."

"Do you remember the first time you kissed Mandy's mother?"

His muscles tensed and his mouth went dry. He hadn't expected her to swing the conversation to *him*. He inhaled deeply and thought back to that night.

In his life he'd dated a lot of beautiful women, but Jessica had been the most gorgeous, ever. He'd read restaurant reviews to find the best place to take her to dinner. Then they'd gone dancing. After a bottle of wine with their meal, and several drinks at the club, they were both more than a little tipsy when he held her close on the dance floor and made his first moves.

"Yeah. I remember."

"It must have been good."

"Actually, it was average." At the time he'd blamed the booze. Certainly they'd gone on to have some very good sex together. "I guess that should have told me something, huh?"

He reached over to touch her hair again. She had so much of it and the color was so intense. He wondered what it would look like splayed over a bedroom pillow.

"Nick? Why are you pulling my hair?"

"It's an interesting color."

"It's a horrible color."

"Why would you think that?"

"Because I have terrible hair. It never does what I want it to do. I always look like I just stuck my finger in a light socket."

"The problem is you fight your hair. You should learn to go with it."

"What?"

"Go with it, Bridge. Let it flow and curl and don't keep…tying it down the way you usually do."

With her wild hair and mysterious eyes, she really wasn't ordinary looking at all. It had just taken him a while to notice, because she didn't fish for compliments, didn't flirt, didn't tease.

And yet she was turning him on right now in a new and different way he couldn't quite understand.

"Bridge?"

"Yes?"

"What do you think it would be like if *we* kissed? Do you think in five years you'd forget all about it the way you did with Troy?"

"Probably."

Oh, she was a funny girl. "Is that a dare?"

"Maybe."

He thought she was holding her breath, waiting to see what he would do. And what would he do? Just a few minutes ago he'd been congratulating himself on spending a platonic evening with an attractive woman.

But he should have known himself better than that.

He let go of her hair and moved his hand until he was cupping the back of her head. He was going to kiss this woman. Kiss her and make sure she remembered it, always.

CHAPTER NINE

BRIDGET'S LIPS WERE sweet and soft, unadorned with any gloss or lipstick. As Nick settled his mouth over hers, she parted her lips, just the right amount, at just the right angle. He felt immediate connection. Immediate heat.

Their tongues met and the connection deepened. Heat became fire. He had to touch her. That wonderful hair. The back of her neck. The curve of her waist.

He pulled back for just a second. Her eyes were closed, cheeks and lips pink as candy floss. "Bridget…you surprise me."

He kissed her again, not so gentle this time, yearning to get closer, deeper. And with every move, Bridget followed, as if this was somehow choreographed. How else could she fit so perfectly next to him—her breath and his, there was no difference.

The kiss was supposed to be one that Bridget would always remember. It turned out to be one Nick would never forget. The second time he parted from her, she let out a ragged sigh that had him picturing naked skin on clean, white linens.

Slow down, warned the sane part of his brain. *This is way too much, way too soon.*

In Nick's experience, nothing was as unique as the way a woman kissed. If the chemistry didn't work with a kiss, it wouldn't work in bed, either.

With Bridget, he hadn't expected to feel such an instant, hot connection. But there was passion in her, as well as sweetness, and the combination was incredibly powerful. And seductive.

It took a long time for reason to return. To gain the upper hand. Finally, when he was able, he gently disengaged.

Enough. Yes, she was a single, available woman. But this was not what he had come here for. He was here for peace, not madness, and surely kissing Bridget Humphrey like this was madness.

Still, as he released her, he couldn't resist brushing his fingers over her cheek and down the side of her neck. She leaned into his touch, as if she craved it. Her intriguing green eyes held a hint of a question. But whatever she was wondering, she didn't ask. Instead she cleared her throat.

"Interesting," she said.

"Very." She didn't say whether his was a kiss worth remembering and he didn't ask. He found he couldn't keep up the teasing tone from before.

Settling back into the cushions—not as far away from her as before, but not too close either—he tried to focus on the movie again. They'd missed a good chunk of the middle, but they both knew the story so well it didn't matter.

At one point he got up to check on Mandy.

"How is she?"

"Sleeping soundly." He returned to the sofa, a safe distance from Bridget and tried again to get into the story on the screen. But he was so tired his eyes were burning and he couldn't think straight.

How did anyone with a baby manage to hold down a job without losing their mind? He wondered how much longer Mandy would sleep until she woke up crying. So far she hadn't gone for much longer than two or three hours. He'd left the door to her room open to make sure he would hear her. Hopefully, though, she would sleep until the end of the movie. Bridget seemed to be really enjoying it.

He squinted at the screen. Jimmy Stewart was getting desperate about the missing money. He had to stay awake, at least until the end...

KISSING NICK had been amazing. But obviously it hadn't affected him the same way, or he wouldn't have stopped so abruptly.

Bridget was sure that checking on his daughter was just an excuse to move farther away from her on the couch. Was he worried she would read too much into that kiss?

If so, why had he kissed her in the first place? The lead up to the kiss had been playful and fun. No preparation at all for the raw passion she'd felt when his lips touched hers.

This, she'd understood immediately, was why she hadn't been able to marry Troy, or Brett, either. This spontaneous combustion of male and female was something she'd read about but had never experienced in real life.

She was glad now that she hadn't settled, but totally bewildered by what should happen next. Nick was acting so nonchalant. She did her best to do the same.

Focus on the movie, she told herself. *It's your favorite, remember?* She was finally getting back into the mood when she felt something brush her shoulder.

Nick. Had he moved closer? She didn't dare turn her head to look, but suddenly the pictures on the screen had no meaning for her. She couldn't think about anything but the point of contact between him and her.

What did this mean? She didn't know. But if just a little touch could affect her this strongly, what would it be like if they actually—

Bridget sighed when he touched her shoulder again. This time, though, it wasn't just a touch.

He was leaning. Quite heavily.

"Nick?" She couldn't resist; she had to look at him.

And when she did, she almost laughed. He was fast asleep. He hadn't leaned into her, he'd fallen. And she'd thought he was about to get all hot and heavy.

Gently she pulled away, letting him sink into the cushions. She turned off the television, then settled a blanket over his muscular, fit body.

The couch was oversize, so he would be comfortable enough. If he wasn't, he could always get up and move to the spare room. He knew where it was, but she dimmed the hallway light and left it on, just in case.

NICK OPENED his eyes. Was it his imagination or could he smell coffee? He tried to roll over but couldn't.

He was on a couch. Bridget's couch.

He checked his watch. It was past eight. Eight? What had happened to Mandy?

He pushed his body up, planted his feet on the floor. He was halfway to the spare room when Bridget's voice stopped him.

"She's still sleeping," she said quietly.

He peeked around the corner into the kitchen. Bridget was putting a tray into the oven. Usually she wore loose-fitting skirts and long sweaters, but this morning she was dressed in yoga pants and a long-sleeved shirt that clung to her rounded breasts. He remembered their kiss and was instantly turned-on.

Coffee. He needed coffee. He went to the pot on the counter. "Mind if I help myself?"

"Please do."

He filled a mug sitting next to the pot, then, noticing her mug was half-empty, topped it up, too. "What time was Mandy up in the night? I'm sorry I didn't hear her." He felt badly that Bridget's sleep had been disturbed, but God did it feel good to get a solid night of sleep himself. Even if it was on a couch.

"She hasn't made a peep since we tucked her in at nine."

He couldn't believe it. "She hasn't slept through the night once since Jessica left."

"Maybe she finally reached the point of exhaustion."

"She wasn't the only one." He tried to remember when he'd fallen asleep. It must have been during the movie. Shortly after that kiss.

The kiss had been way better than he could have imagined. But how did Bridget feel about it? She didn't seem any different. At least she wasn't angry.

"Look, I'm sorry about last night. Falling asleep on the couch. That was pretty rude."

"You were tired. It's okay, Nick."

"And before that—kissing you." Her cheeks turned pink and for some reason he found that cute. "I made a game out of it, and I shouldn't have. You're too nice of a person."

The pink darkened to red. Bridget turned her back on him as she reached for a basket from the cupboard. "It's okay," she said, still not looking at him. "Don't worry about it."

"All right." That hadn't gone over well, he suspected, but not much he could do about it now without belaboring the point. Nick took his coffee to the kitchen table and found the Sunday paper rolled up in front of him. He slipped off the elastic, then remembered his manners.

"Can I help with anything?"

Bridget was now cutting fruit. "No thanks."

"You're not going to all this trouble for me, I hope. I don't usually eat much breakfast."

"I do."

"Okay, then." He opened the paper and sipped the

coffee. After an awkward few minutes had passed, he began to read aloud a few of the news items and Bridget made the occasional comment.

He had just finished with the paper when the alarm on the stove cut him off. Bridget removed a tray of muffins. She tipped them into a basket, then placed it on the table along with a bowl of fruit salad.

"I know you don't eat much for breakfast," she said as she joined him at the table, "but if you change your mind, feel free to help yourself."

He gave her a sheepish grin and went for a muffin. "They do smell good."

They tasted even better. When he was done, he sat back in his chair and tried to remember the last time he'd felt this good. "Thanks for letting us crash for the night, Bridge. We should settle up for the week. I'll pay you double time for yesterday and last night—"

She shook her head. "I'll charge you for the regular hours. But Saturday was a favor. And I won't take money for last night. I didn't do anything. Mandy slept the entire time."

"But, I want to pay you. It's only fair."

"Well, you can't. I don't work weekends. It's a firm policy with me." She picked up the newspaper. "I take it there wasn't anything in here about Tara?"

"Not a word. I want to phone in and check if there were any developments overnight."

"Good idea."

Bridget left the room to go to the bathroom and he took the opportunity to call the station. When she returned with her hair in a ponytail, he answered the silent question on her face. "Nothing new."

"I'm not sure whether to be disappointed or glad."

He knew what she meant.

"What's your next step?"

He shook his head wearily. "Go back to the beginning and make sure we haven't missed anything. Interview her classmates and her teachers again, though I don't expect it will do any good."

"Why?"

"Well—" he hated to admit it, but "—I think you were right about Tara being a misfit. The kids on that list her parents gave me aren't friends. Reading between the lines, I'd guess that some of them spent time with her because of parental pressure. You know, the parents are friends so they expect the kids to feel the same way about each other."

"I know."

Something in her voice caught his attention. "You say that like you've had some experience."

"Never mind about me. Tell me more about Tara."

"That's just it. There is no more. If Tara isn't with a friend, then where the hell is she? Let's say she was angry at her folks and left on impulse. Where would a kid like her go?"

"Tara's naive, not stupid. I can't see her leaving home unless she had a plan."

"So she's not wandering the streets?"

"I don't think so."

Was he crazy to believe her? "I hope you're right about that."

"Even if I am, I don't think it's necessarily good news. Tara would only go with someone she trusted. But Nick—what if she trusted the wrong person?"

He tried to wrap his mind around what she was saying. "We didn't find any evidence of an online predator."

"So it has to be someone she knows."

"We've already established she was a loner."

"Yes, which would make her an easy target for an older, more experienced man."

Nick swore as he thought about a case his brother had been involved with last year. Matt's son's soccer coach had been accused of sexual interference with a minor. The case had been complicated and ugly and an innocent young girl had suffered terribly.

It was conceivable that something similar had happened to Tara. "Tara had several male teachers. And a swimming instructor," he remembered. "I'll make a point of interviewing them again as soon as possible."

"The man could even be a family friend," Bridget said. "Someone her parents trust too much to ever suspect."

"I'll get a list of everyone who has visited the house in the past couple months." It was a long shot but at least gave him something to work on.

"It's worth a try. Nick, something else I think we should try…"

We?

"…I know this is going to sound crazy to you, but if you could give me a list of names and birth dates of these men, I might be able to help you focus your investigation on a few individuals."

"You're right. It sounds crazy."

"Nick—"

"I'm a cop, okay? Just because I humored you and discussed your theories, doesn't mean I'm suddenly a big believer here."

"Humored me?" Bridget flung her head higher and narrowed her eyes. "I thought we were having a productive conversation here. I thought I was *helping*."

"Bridget, this is what I'm trained to do, okay? Like it or not, this is *my* case. Not yours."

"Fine. Stand on your pride. Don't worry about closing doors when you could be helping Tara."

She was pushing *his* buttons now. As if he wouldn't do *anything* in the realm of the possible to find that girl. "What you're asking is *impossible*. The Hartford Police Department doesn't have 'take a friend to work' day."

"I didn't say I had to meet these people. I just want names and dates of birth."

"Bridget, you'll be wasting your time—"

"I helped one of my clients figure out which of his employees was stealing from him. And I don't want to tell you how many married men and women have found out their spouses were cheating—"

"Okay." He held up his hand like a traffic cop. He didn't need to hear all this. He had no faith in numerology, but in his line of work he'd run across some people who were born with a natural intuitiveness and he wouldn't be surprised if Bridget was one of them.

"I'll bring you the list, okay?"

She nodded, and an uneasy silence settled over the room. It didn't last long, though. A familiar baby's cry tore Nick's thoughts from the case back to his daughter.

Mandy was awake. And it sounded like she wanted everyone on the block to know it.

ON SUNDAYS Nick usually got together with his family. Since Gavin had moved to New Hampshire, this meant his mother and Matt and, depending on whether or not he had custody that weekend, Matt's kids Derrick and Violet. Now that Matt was remarried, it meant Jane, too.

Sometimes they met for brunch, but today the plans were for dinner, in the big new home Matt and Jane had purchased shortly after their wedding.

Nick drove to the classic Cape Cod house, with Mandy buckled into her car seat. She seemed happy and he wondered if she knew they were going to visit her cousins. He'd noticed before that Mandy was fascinated by Derrick and Violet. At family gatherings she watched them ceaselessly.

At the house, Nick unloaded Mandy and her baby gear, handing the pink diaper bag to his sister-in-law with a grimace. "One of these days I'm going to get rid of that thing."

"Good idea, Nick. I'm not sure if they make black leather diaper bags, though," Jane teased.

"Anything would be better than *pink*. Hey, buddy!" He gave his nephew a high five, then scooped up Violet with his free arm. His four-year-old niece was a real beauty, with a disposition just as sweet.

Nick walked inside that way, with Violet in one arm, and Mandy in the other. When they got to the family room, Mandy reached for the dollhouse Violet had obviously been playing with. He set the two girls down.

"Don't let her put anything small in her mouth," he warned Violet.

"I'll keep an eye on them," Jane promised.

Nick found his mother in the kitchen, supervising Matt as he removed their dinner from foil containers provided by Red Tree Catering.

Despite the painful ending to his first marriage, Matt was now happy. Nick grinned at the sight of his cerebral brother dealing with serving dishes and ovens, a look of absolute contentment on his face.

A former workaholic, Matt had quit the law firm where Jane still worked in order to practice independently. Now, as he transferred roast potatoes to a heavy clay casserole dish, their mother looked up from the itemized invoice stapled to one of the three brown paper bags sitting on the kitchen table.

"I can't believe how much you paid for this dinner, Matthew."

"It doesn't matter, Mom. The money's well spent for the amount of hassle we saved."

"Next week I should come over and cook for everyone."

"And give up Sunday afternoon bridge?"

Their mother colored and Nick and Matt laughed.

"Time is money, Mom," Matt said. "Buying dinner tonight allowed Jane to go into the office and me to take the kids sledding at the park."

Later, at the table, their mom conceded that the food from the caterer—though outrageously expensive—was at least delicious. "They always overcook roast beef at our place," she said, referring to the senior complex where she'd lived the past several years. "But this is done to perfection."

Matt winked at Nick.

Once the meal was finished and everyone had lingered over pie and coffee, Nick cleared the plates. Since he rarely hosted family get-togethers, he always assigned himself kitchen duty after the meal. Sometimes Matt joined him so they could have a chance to talk. In the past, he and Matt had tended to butt heads quite a bit. The hard times they'd all been through lately…Sam's death, Matt's divorce, and then Nick's, had changed their outlooks.

These days they were both trying a little harder to get along.

"So how's it going looking after Mandy full time?"

"Way harder than I thought. Especially the nights. Man, I've never been so tired in my life. Not even when I worked the night shift."

"I remember those years," Matt said, sounding nostalgic.

Probably his kids had slept through to morning soon after they were born. It still worried Nick that Mandy woke up so often in the night when she was with him. She didn't do that with Jessica and she hadn't at Bridget's.

What further proof did he need of his inadequacies as a father?

"What are you doing with Mandy when you go to work?"

"I've been leaving her with the neighborhood dog-sitter."

"*Dog*-sitter?"

"Turns out Bridget is great with babies, too. Frankly, she's saving my butt."

"Bridget, huh? How old is this dog and baby-sitting woman?"

"I don't know. Maybe late twenties."

"Good-looking?"

"I guess. But not my type."

"Really?" Matt looked curious but, with newfound tact, didn't ask anything more about her. "So how much longer is your butt going to need saving?"

"Until a week after Christmas."

"I'm surprised Jessica would leave Mandy for so long."

"Hey, it was a once-in-a-lifetime chance to see Australia," he said, his tone mocking.

"Babies change a lot in three weeks. She might come home to the realization that the trip wasn't worth the price."

Nick knew his brother was speaking from his own painful experience. For too many years Matt had put his work obligations ahead of the needs of his family. His relationship with his son had suffered as a result. But the damage hadn't been irreparable.

"Derrick says you've agreed to be assistant coach to his soccer team next spring."

Matt nodded.

"Good decision. Leaving Brandstrom and Norton has sure been the right thing for you, hasn't it?" He'd never seen his brother happier than the past six months.

"Yeah. I'd say I have my priorities straight for the first time in my life. How about you? Have you thought about what's going to happen when Jessica returns?"

"A little," he admitted. "One thing's for sure. We can't go back to the way things were before."

"You going to ask for more time with Mandy?"

"I'd like to. Jessica always said Mandy was too young to spend the night with me, but obviously that argument won't hold water anymore."

"So you're going to have Mandy on weekends? Are you sure your love life can handle the shock?"

Nick knew he was being teased, but he couldn't muster a responding grin. "My love life isn't much of an issue these days."

Matt gave him his most probing defense-attorney look. "Short on free time since the promotion to detective?"

"That's part of it." He hesitated, then decided if he couldn't trust his brother, who could he trust? "I haven't felt like dating anyone since Jessica moved out."

"That's not like you."

"Don't I know it. But I'm just not interested."

Matt folded his arms across his chest. "Your priorities have changed, too. You have a daughter now so you see the world differently. It's only natural."

Was Matt right? Was that what was happening to him? Surely one day, though, he'd want to start going out with women again.

He thought of Bridget. The way he felt whenever he was with her. It was a good feeling, but it wasn't the giddy excitement he usually experienced when he met a new woman he wanted to date.

No giddy excitement, huh? What about that kiss?

Forget the kiss. That didn't count. He'd been super tired and it had been a long time since he'd been with a woman. Pent-up hormones were what had made that kiss so great.

"Maybe I'm not cut out to be a family man the way you and Gavin are."

"To hell with that. When the right woman comes along, you'll feel different."

That was the way it had been for his brothers. They'd both had rocky first relationships, too, but had settled down happily once Allison and Jane came into the picture.

Nick flexed the hand where he'd worn his wedding ring so briefly. If only it could be that straightforward for him.

CHAPTER TEN

AT THE BRIEFING on Monday morning Nick stood with Glenn at the back of the room. Chief Wilson wasn't happy. Vincent Lang had called on the weekend expressing his disappointment with the lack of progress in finding his daughter.

"We are still operating on the assumption that the girl is a runaway, hiding with friends somewhere in Hartford. We've come up with nothing that suggests otherwise."

Nothing, Nick thought, but the opinion of the numerologist who was babysitting his daughter. He wished he could scoff at Bridget's ideas, but unfortunately his own hunches were leading him the same way. He had to speak up. "Given the amount of time that has passed, shouldn't we consider the possibility that Tara Lang may have been the target of a sexual predator?"

"On what basis would we say this? Do you have a theory, Gray?"

"Abduction doesn't seem likely. Not considering all the stuff she took with her. But she could have been coerced or lured into leaving."

"By who?"

"Someone she trusted. A family friend. Someone she met at the pool or online. A teacher."

The Chief of Detectives looked at him skeptically, then let out a frustrated breath. "Well, I guess it wouldn't hurt for you and Glenn to explore that avenue." He pointed to another team of detectives. "Lawson, Michaels, I want you to talk to all the kids on that list the parents gave us. Make sure they've told you everything they know. And the rest of you keep your eyes peeled. If she's out on the street, like I think she is, we're going to spot her sooner or later."

Again, Nick felt compelled to speak. "Maybe it's time we sent out an appeal through the media."

This time the Chief's glare was withering. "Yeah, why don't you try talking Vincent Lang into that plan? Our attorney general only cares about one thing and that's having his daughter back by this Sunday afternoon without the public ever having known that she was gone."

"Why Sunday?" one of the officers asked.

"The mayor's Christmas skating party is on Sunday. It's an important photo op," he added, his tone as dry as the mayor's party was sure to be.

NICK AND GLENN DROVE to the pool first. Tara Lang had taken her lessons at her parents' private club. The administrator was very cooperative when they asked for her help. The woman, in her early thirties with her light brown hair in a sporty ponytail, gave them a list of the lifeguards and instructors who would have known Tara.

"We're happy to cooperate with the police department," she said, her smile sunny. "Can you tell me what this is in regards to?"

"We're not at liberty to discuss that right now, miss," Nick said very properly.

Glenn poked him in the ribs when the administrator wasn't looking. "Very smooth," he said with a grin.

Nick ignored him. As the days passed by, he couldn't help getting more invested in this case. This girl was just fourteen. He wanted her found. And, preferably, he wanted to be the guy who found her.

One of the instructors, twenty-year-old Morgan Keenan, was available to talk with them right then. Based on the name, Nick had expected a guy, but it was very much a young woman who came off the pool deck to talk to them. She was tall, with an athletic, broad-shouldered body. She had a pair of sweatpants over her one-piece bathing suit, and had rolled the waistband down to her hips. Her blond hair was dry but slicked back from her face.

"You had some questions?" She looked from Nick to Glenn, then back to Nick.

"Why don't you sit down?" Nick pulled out a chair. The administrator had been helpful enough to offer them use of her office.

"Denise said this was about Tara Lang?"

"How well did you know her?" Glenn asked.

"I was her swim instructor last session." Morgan's eyes were bright and inquisitive. "I heard a rumor that she's in some sort of trouble."

Glenn didn't respond and she turned to Nick. "Do you think something bad happened to her?"

"Why do you ask that? Did she talk to you about any problems she was having?"

"No. We weren't friends or anything."

"Did Tara have friends in the class?"

"Mostly she stuck to herself. She was pretty quiet."

A misfit at the pool as well as at school, Nick concluded. "Did she like to swim? Was she good at it?"

Morgan shrugged. "Lots of kids enroll in swimming lessons because their parents make them. For safety reasons mostly, so they won't have to worry when their kids hang out at the pool or the lake. I'd say Tara definitely fell into this category."

"So she took swimming lessons but didn't enjoy them?" Glenn confirmed.

Morgan glanced at him briefly and nodded before turning back to Nick. She crossed her legs, then tilted her head. "I'm sorry I can't be more help. But maybe I'll think of something later. Do you have a number where I could reach you?"

She was flirting, Nick realized, belatedly. Trying not to betray his amusement with a smile, he nodded in Glenn's direction. "I forgot my cards today, buddy. Do you have one on you?"

Glenn did and he passed it to the girl, who didn't hide her disappointment. He pretended not to notice. "If you do think of anything, please call right away."

"I will." She gave Nick one last look, then left the office.

Glenn waited a few seconds before he let out a deep laugh. "Holy crap, man, how do you do it?"

"Stop it. She's just a kid."

"Twenty is not a kid. Did you see the way she looked at you?"

Nick shrugged. "I'm not interested." He stood and grabbed his jacket. "We're finished here. Time to head to the school."

Glenn put on his coat, too, but he refused to let the subject of the young woman drop. "She was young, pretty and hot. Why wouldn't you want to give her your number?"

"I'm too old."

"Bull. I'm not too old to be interested and I've got fifteen years on you."

More like twenty. Nick opened the door, waiting for his partner to precede him out of the office. Once he would have given that young swim instructor his business card, no doubt about it.

"I've got a daughter now, Glenn. Things have changed." But it wasn't Mandy's smile he was picturing as he climbed into the car. It was Bridget's.

AT HIS FIRST VISIT to Tara's private school, the principal had assured Nick that he and his staff would assist in every possible way with the police investigation into Tara's absence. He'd also promised the utmost in discretion. But as Nick made his way to the office this afternoon, he could tell from the whispers and stares around him, that every kid in the building knew Tara Lang was missing.

The principal agreed to let Nick and Glenn use the same room for their interviews as they'd used last time. Shortly after the door had been unlocked for them, an administrative assistant brought them a thermos of coffee, two mugs and some shortbread cookies.

"I love these swank private schools," Glenn said as he filled his mug with the richly scented brew.

This was the second time the teachers had been questioned about Tara Lang's disappearance and they each reacted to the pressure in different ways.

Tara's social studies teacher seemed concerned, but clearly anxious to get back to her class since, in her opinion, she didn't have anything useful to tell them.

The überfit man who taught Tara P.E. appeared nervous, stammering a few times and contradicting himself in minor details.

The math and science teachers were calm and collected. Both were male and none had any additional information to offer.

"This kid has been in their classrooms since September," Glenn said, in a lull between interviews. "And yet none of these clowns really knew her."

"It's frustrating," Nick agreed. They couldn't put it down to the large number of students. In this posh school, each classroom held less than twenty kids.

The only teacher who seemed to have made any connection with Tara at all was Colin Porter who taught English.

"She's a very sensitive girl," he told them. "A talented writer, though she was too shy to share her work with the class."

"That would explain why she earned A's in English when all her other grades were C's," Nick said.

Colin nodded. He was a slight man, but nice-looking, with a narrow, fine-featured face and short brown hair.

"Did she ever talk to you about problems she was having at home?"

"I was asked this question before," Colin said patiently. "The answer is still no. As I've already said, Tara is a very private girl. She doesn't share personal information easily."

How would he know that, Nick wondered. Just because she hadn't shared personal information with him? Few kids that age would confide their problems to a teacher.

"Did Tara seem happy to you?" he asked.

"Not overly. But a lot of kids in my classes are rather moody. I'd like to think it's the age and not my teaching," he added with a smile.

A charmer, Nick noted. "Anything else you can tell us about her?"

"She loves analyzing the poetry in songs and, when given a writing assignment, prefers to write in verse. I realize this probably isn't very helpful to you and I'm sorry." He leaned forward, his expression earnest. "I hope you find her soon."

"We're doing our best." He gave Porter a brief smile, glad that at least one of Tara's teachers had taken the time to get to know her.

As Nick and Glenn drove back to the station, they discussed their impressions of the people they'd interviewed. They both agreed that they had nothing to follow up with the next day.

Very frustrating.

Back at the department, they checked in with the dispatcher, then went to see to their Captain. Harper's expression was flat during their report but when he spoke his voice was snarly. "Nothing new. Not a single lead. What the hell am I going to report to the Chief when he calls me into his office in two hours?"

"Maybe you can convince him it's time to ask for help from the public?"

The Captain gave Nick a "get real" look. Then he flicked his hand at them. "Beat it. Come back when you've got something that will put a smile on my face for a change."

What am I missing, Nick wondered as he headed back to his desk to check his mail and tidy his desk. The kid wasn't that sophisticated. She shouldn't be this difficult to find.

Before Mandy had come to stay with him, Nick had often worked until six or later. Now, despite his urge to keep digging for a new lead, he closed down the computer and locked his desk. As he prepared to leave, he realized he wasn't just looking forward to seeing Mandy, but Bridget, too. Since he'd kissed her he'd been thinking of her too often. He'd kissed a lot of women over the years. Why did this one kiss and this one woman seem so different?

"By the way, you've got me curious about something," Glenn said, when he saw Nick slip on his jacket to head home.

"What?"

"Everyone we talked to today—you asked for their birth date. What was that about?"

Nick shrugged. "Nothing important. See you later, Glenn. Maybe tomorrow will be our lucky day."

"BEFORE YOU ASK," Nick said, tromping snow into the foyer, "We didn't find her."

Bridget—sitting cross-legged on the floor wrapping Christmas gifts by the tree—hadn't bothered to get up to answer the door, figuring since it was unlocked, Nick could let himself in. All her dogs had been picked up already, except Lefty. He and Mandy were dozing on the white rug, surrounded by strands of ribbons and wads of shiny paper.

"Bad day, huh?" she asked. He sounded grumpy. Even so, when he stepped into the room, she felt as if the lights on the tree dimmed just a little in comparison. He had an energy, a vibe that couldn't be ignored.

The scowl on his face softened when he spotted his daughter. She was curled up beside Lefty, one of her hands resting on the boxer's paw.

"She wouldn't take her nap today," Bridget said softly. "So I kept her with me while I wrapped some presents. She was happy for a long while, playing with the paper and the ribbons. Then about fifteen minutes ago, Lefty settled beside her and they both sort of drifted off together."

"They look cute."

"Don't they? Lefty adores her and I think the feeling is mutual."

"Where are the other dogs?"

"They've gone home already. Lefty's owner often picks him up late. Elizabeth is a corporate VP and works horrendous hours."

"Poor Lefty."

"At least Elizabeth brings him to doggy day care and doesn't leave him alone in her condo all day."

"Good point." Nick surveyed the small pile under the tree, then frowned. "Some of these are for Mandy."

"Yes." And one of them was for him. A navy replacement for that pink diaper bag he despised so much. "Have you started your Christmas shopping yet?"

He made a face. "I usually buy gift certificates."

"Not for Mandy, surely."

"She won't know the difference. Not this Christmas. Look, you may enjoy putting up a tree, baking cookies and all that holiday tripe, but I've got more important worries. Like finding Tara Lang."

He crouched and touched his daughter's cheek gently. "And taking care of my daughter."

She couldn't argue with that point.

As Nick stroked Mandy's hair, the look on his face was so tender that Bridget's heart welled in response.

She recalled how it had felt to have him touch her and kiss her. She'd replayed those exquisite moments in her mind often since they'd happened. Sometimes she wondered if their kiss really had been as fabulous as she remembered. Because, if it had, how was Nick able to act as if nothing had happened between them?

Either he was a much better actor than her, or he hadn't felt the same magic.

She was probably lucky he hadn't sucked her into a full-blown affair. A man like Nick could tear her apart in ways her previous, nice-but-unexciting boy-friends had not.

"Nick, would you—" The phone interrupted her before she could ask if he wanted a drink. She hurried to grab the portable receiver, but not before the jarring noise woke Mandy. The baby started crying just as she hit the talk button.

"It's okay, sweetie." Nick picked her up, stroked her head.

Bridget moved to the far side of the room, shield-ing the mouthpiece with her hand. "Hello?"

"Bridget, this is Annabel."

"How are you doing?" As the days had passed by with no sign of Tara, Bridget had been expecting another call from the girl's mother.

"Terrible. I've been living a nightmare, Bridget. The last time we spoke I wasn't completely honest with you. But now I need to see you as soon as possible."

Her schedule was full for the rest of the week, but she'd make room for Annabel. "When would you like to come?"

"Later tonight. Is that possible?" Annabel's voice wavered. Clearly she'd been crying. "Vincent has a function. I need to be at the dinner, but I can slip out around nine. Is that too late?"

"No, it will be fine." She offered a few encourag-ing words to Annabel before disconnecting. As she placed the phone on a nearby table, she noticed Nick eyeing her with that detective gaze of his.

"Annabel Lang?"

She hadn't mentioned any name. The man's instincts were impeccable. "Yes."

"She's booked an appointment?" His eyes were still focused on her as he jiggled Mandy gently in his arms. The baby had calmed and was now half-dozing, with her head nestled against her daddy's chest.

Bridget hesitated, then nodded. As she jotted the appointment into the book she kept near the phone, she sensed Nick looking over her shoulder.

He seemed curious. "What are your clients like? Mostly rich, lonely women like Annabel Lang?"

How had he known Annabel was lonely? "My clients are a cross-section of regular people. Some women, some men. Some wealthy, some just average. What they have in common is a desire to maximize the potential in their lives. They are people who like to plan and prepare. To be proactive rather than reactive."

"And you help them by telling them what's in their future so they can prepare for it. But what about when you're wrong? Don't they get disillusioned?"

"You are so off base. Numerology isn't about predicting the future. Most people live their lives without any awareness. It's like taking a car trip across the country but not taking a map. You really should let me calculate your life path number. You might be surprised what you could learn about yourself."

"Don't get started on that again." He pulled a sheet of paper from the front pocket of his jeans. "I'm not a believer. I'll never be a believer. But I got you those names and dates you asked for. Don't ask me why."

He slapped the paper down on her table. "Knock yourself out with it."

She ignored his rudeness and glanced over the list. The names themselves had an energy, an aura. As she read each one, she made note of her immediate reaction. Later she would do the necessary calculations to see if she could pinpoint any potential suspects.

She didn't care about impressing Nick. All she wanted was to find Tara.

As she ran her eyes over the names again, she felt Nick step up behind her.

"Want me to tell you about them?"

"It isn't necessary." She could feel his solid warmth behind her. If she leaned back even a few inches, her body would meet his. She imagined the sensation of his arm sliding around her waist and pulling her close.

She closed her eyes and waited for him to move away. For the longest time he didn't. Then, abruptly he asked for Mandy's snowsuit and five minutes later he and his daughter were gone.

She stood at the kitchen window for a bit, watching them go, aware of a complex surge of emotions. Just last week she would have admitted to a having a bit of a crush on Nick Gray. But her feelings for him were getting deeper with every day. Falling for him—seriously risking her heart—would be a disaster in every way.

But she just couldn't seem to stop herself.

CHAPTER ELEVEN

ON TUESDAY MORNING Nick had a message waiting from Tara's mother. Annabel Lang wanted to meet with him right away and suggested a coffee shop near Bushnell Park. Before leaving the department, Nick called Bridget. He caught her just before she was about to leave with Mandy and the dogs for a walk.

"Guess who wants to talk with me today?"

"Sorry, Nick. I don't predict the future and I can't read minds, either."

"Ouch. Guess I deserved that. It's your client, Annabel Lang. I'm wondering if something you said to her last night resulted in her requesting this meeting today. Care to fill me in?"

After a pause, Bridget said carefully, "That's for Annabel to tell you. Not me."

Damn. "Don't tell me numerologists worry about client confidentiality." Maybe he'd gone too far that time. "That wasn't called for. Sorry. I'm just—"

"You just can't take me, or what I do, seriously. I get it, Nick. Good luck with Annabel. Go easy on her. She's had a tough week."

Bridget disconnected and Nick was left staring

at his phone. He hadn't handled that conversation very well, he decided. Pocketing the phone, he grabbed his notebook then headed for the café. He arrived ten minutes early and was able to snag a seat near the back with an unobstructed view of the front door.

The coffee shop teemed with people anxious for their morning fix. A constant lineup snaked between the counter and the tables at the front of the café. Mostly professional men and women in suits, though one young man in fluorescent biking attire stood out from the rest. He had a courier's logo across the pack on his back.

Idly, Nick wondered what important documents were being delayed in their delivery so the cyclist could get his shot of caffeine.

At five minutes past the hour she'd arranged for their meeting, Annabel Lang entered the café. She was wearing a fitted black coat, with fur on the collar, and carried a large pink leather purse. Probably a big designer-name bag, Nick thought, though he didn't recognize the initials stamped on the side.

He stood and waved her over. He had two coffees waiting on the table, but was prepared to get her something else if she wanted.

"The lineup is so long. This will do." She perched on the second chair, keeping her purse on her lap.

Today she looked like a mother whose daughter was missing. The whites of her eyes were pink and lines etched around her mouth and forehead clearly broadcast her age, despite a modest application of makeup.

She let out her breath and her shoulders sank a few inches.

At their first meeting Nick had taken a slight dislike to the woman. Today all he could feel was sympathy.

"Seven days. An entire week."

He had to ask, even though the answer was obvious. "You haven't heard anything?"

"Not a word."

He thought about his nephew, who was only a year younger than Tara. If Derrick had been missing for a week, he'd be going crazy. And Matt—he'd be a wild man, Nick was sure.

"Do you still think she's hiding out at a friend's house?"

Annabel Lang shook her head sadly. "I wish I could hang on to that hope, but I can't. Maybe she could pull off a stunt like that for a few days. But not this long."

"I tend to agree."

"But then where is she? On the street?" Tara's mother blinked rapidly to stem the tears.

Nick wondered if being out on the street was the worst fate she could imagine for her daughter. "It's possible. In which case it might be time to make an appeal to the public. Our guys are searching for her, Mrs. Lang. But the more eyes on the lookout the better."

She nodded. "That's what I'd like to do. But Vincent is against that plan. He still thinks this is some sort of prank that Tara is pulling."

Anger flashed briefly in her eyes and Nick felt his

own antagonism toward the attorney general harden. What would it take for this guy to show some genuine concern for his daughter?

A trip to the morgue?

"You could go public by yourself."

Her eyes widened at the idea. For a second she seemed to consider the option. But then she shook her head. "There has to be something else we can do. Do you have any ideas, Detective? I'll do anything to help. Anything but that."

Anything but the one thing with any probability of being effective. Nick tried to disguise his impatience. Annabel wasn't the culprit here, even though her inability to stand up to her husband was frustrating.

"We're already doing everything we can think of, Mrs. Lang. The force has a lot of people working to find your daughter. Yesterday we had a team of detectives recheck the list of her friends. My partner and I were out at the country club and at her school talking to people. The cops on the street are searching, too."

He wanted to reassure her that every possible effort was being made.

But unfortunately it wasn't.

The one thing that would help the most was the very thing her husband wouldn't let them do.

THE DAY FELT LONG to Nick. Maybe because he couldn't get a break in the Tara Lang case. He had other files that required his attention, but this was the one Captain Harper and Chief Wilson were breathing down his neck about.

After his meeting with Annabel Lang, Nick spent the morning catching up on paperwork and following a few leads over the phone. Around noon, he stretched his legs and went to get a coffee. He passed a coworker who was perusing the classifieds in the *Courant*. One bold heading caught his eye.

Boxer Puppies. Interesting. "Mind if I cut that out?"

"Go ahead."

Nick pocketed the ad, then returned to his desk where he placed a couple of calls. First to the number in the ad, then to his brother, Matt.

When he was done, he went out to grab a sandwich, which he ate in the car. He checked in with Glenn, who'd been called into court that afternoon, then decided to finish off the afternoon by visiting Tara's favorite haunts: the mall, the movie theater, the video store, and a café that sold submarine sandwiches—supposedly Tara's favorite.

All these places were swarming with kids about the same age as Tara. But the missing girl was nowhere to be seen.

By four-thirty Nick was ready to call it a day. He drove home as usual, parking in front of his place, then walked to Bridget's to pick up his daughter.

Bridget came to the door with Mandy in her arms. The sight of the two of them brought a lump to his throat that he had to clear away before he could speak. "Hey, there. How's my little girl?"

He stepped inside and Mandy held out her arms,

leaning her entire body into his. The happiness he felt at holding her close to his heart was almost overwhelming.

Bridget stood watching them, a mushy expression on her face. Like him, she was a softy for babies and dogs. And speaking of which…

"Bridget, I have a favor to ask of you."

"Sounds serious."

"Do you have plans tonight?"

Her brows rose.

"I've been thinking about what you said about buying a gift for Mandy. And I was hoping you'd come shopping with me. Help pick it out."

The hint of confusion disappeared from her eyes and she smiled warmly. "I'm glad. Of course, I'll help. Will we take Mandy with us?"

"Actually my brother has agreed to babysit. We'll drop Mandy off at Matt and Jane's house on the way. Have the dogs been picked up yet?"

"All of them. Even Lefty." Her expression grew serious. "But before we leave can we talk about the list of suspects you gave me yesterday?"

Oh, God. Why had he humored her by providing that list? Now he was going to have to listen to her crackpot ideas. Not wanting to insult her this time, he juggled Mandy from one arm to the next as he removed his boots and coat.

"Let's go to my office," Bridget said, leading the way down the hall.

Her office was the one room he hadn't been inside—apart from her bedroom. He wasn't surprised to find it neat. Scanning the bookshelves he saw volumes on astrology and numerology. But he also saw phrases such as "quantum mechanics" and "string theory" and "relativity," which reminded him of her Harvard past. On the walls were some outstanding photographs of dogs. He recognized Lefty in one of them. A small picture in the corner caught his eye. A young girl with her arms wrapped around a friendly-looking retriever. It wasn't the same quality as the other photographs, but there was a light in the girl's eyes that called to him.

"That's me and Ella. She was a family pet."

The house in the background looked large and impressive. "Your family is rich." The realization was a bit of a shock. Although Harvard should have been enough of a tip-off.

"My parents are academics. Well-off, certainly, but not rich." She waved him to one of two chairs at a corner table. A penciled chart sat atop a pile of papers. To one side he saw the list of names and birth dates he'd left with her last night.

Sitting Mandy on his knee, he took a closer look at the chart. It reminded him a bit of the Spirograph pictures his niece Tory sometimes made. There was a circle divided into twelve segments, each marked by a weird-looking symbol. The center of the circle was filled with criss-crossing lines connecting various points on the circle with one another.

In the top left-hand corner was written Colin Porter's name and birth date followed by some additional numbers he couldn't understand.

"Porter."

Bridget nodded. "He's the one who stands out from the rest. There are definite areas of concern."

She'd picked the one guy he'd interviewed who'd shown genuine concern about Tara.

"Did you check out the gym instructor? He seemed nervous when Glenn and I were interviewing him." Some people got edgy around the police as a matter of course. But there was another reason people reacted that way. It was called guilt.

"I didn't see anything worrisome in his chart."

He processed that. "But you saw something that worried you in Colin Porter's?"

"Yes."

Great. "Let's hear it, then." Mandy reached for a pen on Bridget's desk. After making sure it was closed, he passed it to her.

Despite his skepticism, he was curious to find out what Bridget had to say about Colin. In person the English teacher had been polite, helpful and personable. Nothing about his manner had triggered any of Nick's internal alarms.

"Here's what the numbers have to say about Colin Porter. With a birth date of May second he has a smooth personality, seems to be a good listener and gains trust easily."

Nick nodded. That fit with what he'd seen. But the same could be said about any number of people.

"He's a Taurus with a life path of one. This gives him strong appetites, Nick, and I mean of the sensual variety, not just food."

"He seemed mild mannered in person."

"Did he? Well, I would guess that's a cover. This man has a series of intense five transits, which have the result of exaggerating his sensual needs."

"Sensual, of course, would include sexual?"

She nodded. "That isn't necessarily a problem. Many people can deal with their excessive…appetites…in socially appropriate ways. But people with Colin Porter's life path have a tendency to take what they want without concern for others."

"Not very admirable. But not necessarily a crime."

"It gets worse. What concerns me the most is that he has many number ones but a total lack of sixes."

She sounded so convinced that this was a big deal, it was hard not to take her seriously. "What's that mean?"

"An inability to form loving, caring bonds with other people."

"Like sociopaths."

She nodded.

"But I've met him, Bridget. He comes across like a genuine, nice guy. Of all of Tara's teachers, Colin Porter was the only one who remembered her clearly as a person and not just another body in his classroom. His concern for her welfare seemed very real."

"I'm not surprised he gave you that impression. He is a master at telling people what they want to hear. Did he happen to share any of his impressions about Tara with you?"

Nick pulled out his notebook to help jog his

memory. "He said she was sensitive, a talented writer and shy."

"Did he give Tara good marks in English?"

"Yes. Tara is a C student generally, but in English she earned an A."

"Hmm."

"You think he gave her high marks she didn't deserve?"

"It would help him earn her trust and win her over."

"Or Tara could be one of those kids who suck at science and math but excel in the languages."

"Did she earn good marks in social studies, too?"

"No," he admitted. "But that still doesn't prove anything."

"I didn't expect you to take my reading, go directly to Colin Porter and arrest him."

He had to laugh. "Fair enough."

Bridget didn't smile back. "But I do hope you'll take this seriously enough to question Colin Porter thoroughly. And I mean very thoroughly."

He supposed it wouldn't hurt. "I'll do that tomorrow."

"Thank you. And if I could make one more suggestion?"

"Oh sure. Please do."

She ignored the sarcasm. "Interview him at home, not at the school. I think you'll learn more that way."

He leaned back in his chair and cocked his head as he gazed at her. Despite his skepticism, he was impressed. She definitely sounded like she knew what she was talking about. He could see why some people might get sucked into believing this stuff. But he still couldn't quite understand how *she* could.

"How does a physics major buy into a practice like numerology? I would have thought you'd been trained to think a certain way." Much the way a police officer was trained to think. "To believe in facts and logic and independent verification."

"A lot of very smart people would agree that science doesn't have all the answers." She got up from her chair. "How did your meeting with Annabel go this morning?"

"Not that well. I couldn't talk her into appealing to the public for help finding her daughter. Do you think Tara's parents love her, Bridget?"

"Her mother does," she said. "I have no doubt. And you just wait, Nick. You may have been more persuasive than you think you were."

"What do you mean?"

But Bridget wouldn't say any more. She was damn secretive herself, when she wanted to be.

CHAPTER TWELVE

IN THE CAR Bridget listed some of her ideas for gifts for Mandy. Nick didn't seem to pay any attention to them. So why had he asked her to come shopping with him?

They'd just dropped Mandy off with his brother and wife. Meeting Matthew Gray had been interesting. He seemed so thoroughly domestic and happy with his life. It was hard to believe that he'd once been more married to his career than his family, but Nick had assured her that was the case.

If one brother could change like that…could another do the same?

She glanced at Nick, behind the wheel of his black Camaro. The car spoke volumes about the man. Hot and fast, pleasing to the eye and to the touch. It was the sort of car you knew would be fun for a ride, but not a safe choice for the long haul.

Nick glanced at her and winked, a smile teasing the corner of his mouth. He'd refused to tell her where they were headed or what he wanted to shop for. She didn't really mind. It was enough to see him enjoying himself.

"It's about time you got some Christmas spirit."

He laughed. "Is that what you think this is?"

"What else could it be?"

He didn't answer and, for a moment, Bridget gave in to a daydream where instead of heading to the local mall, Nick whisked her away to a romantic bed-and-breakfast.

A few days ago Nick had promised her a kiss she'd never forget and he'd delivered. What kind of memories could he give her with a whole weekend?

Right. And what kind of heartaches, as well?

She reminded herself of the purpose of this trip. Shopping for Mandy. She looked out the window just in time to spot the turnoff for the mall. But Nick whizzed right by it.

"Weren't we supposed to turn there?"

"I don't think so."

Hmm. What was he up to? He was staring straight ahead, one hand nonchalantly on the wheel, whistling softly, clearly pleased as could be. "You obviously have something specific in mind. So why bring me along?"

"You'll understand when we get there."

"You're trying to frustrate me on purpose."

He flashed her a look that was unabashedly sexual, his gaze openly appraising. "Not at all. My motto is more like, satisfaction guaranteed."

"I'll bet," she muttered, thinking back to the many, many women she'd seen him with over the years.

"Lighten up, Bridge. This is supposed to be fun." He grinned, then said, "You know what I used to love doing the most when I was a kid?"

"Torturing the little girls who lived on your block?"

"Besides that." He concentrated on changing

lanes, then took an exit into a neighborhood she'd never been to before. He reached over to the dash and punched an address into the GPS system. "I used to love going camping with my dad."

Her impatience evaporated. He'd told her his father had died when he was nine. So these memories were from long ago.

"They were great times. Dad, my brothers and me, setting up the tent, then making a fire and roasting hot dogs. During daylight we would fish or go hiking. Such simple stuff. Yet they were the best times."

"I'm glad you have those nice memories of your father." She wouldn't mind a few like that. But her parents were the kind who felt that spare time should be spent on self-improvement. Her holidays had been filled with extra classes and lessons.

He took another corner, then slowed to read the house numbers. "You know what's great to take along with you on a camping trip?"

She'd never been on one, though she guessed she'd probably like it. "A tent. Matches. Sleeping bags."

Nick was smiling again, a dreamy expression on his face. "A dog," he said. Then he stopped the car.

He was out and opening her door before Bridget had finished processing what he'd said. She stepped out to the sidewalk, still vaguely disoriented. She slipped off her sunglasses so she could see his face more clearly. "You want to buy Mandy a dog for Christmas?"

"Great idea, huh? She loves Lefty so much, I thought I'd buy her a boxer. I found this breeder in the paper today."

He started moving briskly for the front door. She stopped him with a hand on his arm. "Wait. Have you thought this through, Nick? Owning a dog is a lot of responsibility."

"A baby is a lot of responsibility," he corrected her. "A dog is a moderate amount of responsibility."

"You still have to feed them, and take care of them and give them lots of love and attention. You have a demanding job. Don't you think your dog will get lonely?"

"I know this great dog-sitter." He touched her under the chin, lifting her face a little.

The touch surprised her, sent a shiver of happiness up her spine. "Actually," she said, "you know a *wonderful* dog-sitter."

"Beautiful, kind and charming in every way," he agreed. "Now can we go look at the puppies, Bridge?"

THEY FELL IN LOVE with all of them, of course. "Look at the fawn-colored one. She's beautiful," Bridget said. But it was a different puppy, one with a white nose and floppy ears, that took a special shine to Nick, and that was the pup that Nick decided he had to have.

"Let's give her another week with her mother," Bridget suggested. That would give Nick plenty of opportunity to reflect on the pros and cons of adding a pet to his already complicated life. They made an agreement with the owner, then returned to the car.

Nick was as excited as a kid. And so was she, actually. "Oh, Nick. I wish we could buy all of them."

"Me, too, though I feel a bit guilty about shopping

for a purebred. My father bought our dog from the humane society. He was just a mutt but he had a really big heart."

"What was his name?"

"We called him Boo because he used to scare so easily. Dad told us he must have had a rough life and we had to be extra kind to him. But Mom never really took to Boo and after Dad died, Boo passed away, too. My brothers tell me I'm crazy, but I think Boo died of a broken heart."

"Oh, Nick. Boo sounds like such a sweetheart. My dog was a purebred. It was the only kind my parents would consider buying."

"You don't talk about your family much. Do your folks live in the city?"

"Yes. But we don't get together often. They don't approve of the choices I've made."

"Which ones?"

"Pretty much all of them. Over the years we've had so many falling-outs. Like when I abandoned my chosen field of physics in order to practice numerology. And when I started the doggy day care—they hated that. They thought my sole motivation was to embarrass them."

Nick said nothing. Probably he thought she had been crazy to change her career so dramatically, too. Certainly the numerology part, anyway.

"Our worst fight happened when I broke up with Troy. My mother actually cried."

"Can't understand why. He didn't seem that great to me."

ON THE DRIVE HOME Nick suggested they stop at the mall to pick up gifts for his nieces and nephews. After fifteen minutes amid the hordes of Christmas shoppers Bridget realized that the real reason for stopping at the mall was so Nick could search for Tara. He spent more time scanning the faces of the passing teenagers than considering the merchandise on display in the stores.

Spotting a bookstore, she steered him to the children's section, but he turned up his nose. "Books are boring gifts."

"They don't have to be." She picked out a rhyming story for preschoolers. The pictures were amazing and the text was clever. "Violet would enjoy this."

"Not bad," Nick agreed. He followed her lead in selecting something for Jack and Tory. Then they moved to the section for teens to hunt for something Derrick might appreciate. Fifteen minutes later, Nick had two full shopping bags and all his gifts had been purchased.

He was leading Bridget out of the store when he stopped abruptly.

"What?" she asked.

He grabbed her arm and leaned his head in closely. "See that girl in the *What's New* section?"

Bridget spotted her right away, a slight girl with spiky dark hair. She could only see her from the back and the hair had been changed, but her instincts told her this was their runaway. "Tara."

"I think so. Stay here while I get a look at her face."

But as Nick moved in closer, the girl seemed to

sense their presence. She turned in their direction and her eyes locked with Nick's, then Bridget's. Emotions flashed over her face. Fear, then recognition, then uncertainty. The book in her hands slid to the floor. The thud seemed to spur her to action. She ran.

Nick tried to follow, but there were several people in the way. By the time he'd navigated around an elderly lady in a walker, Tara was nowhere to be seen. She'd left the store and merged with the crowds in the corridor.

Bridget hurried to catch up with him.

"Did you see which way she went?" he asked. The bookstore was at a crossroads in the mall, so Tara could have headed in any of four directions.

"I couldn't tell. Let's split up and try to find her."

"Do you have your phone?"

When she nodded, he said, "Okay. Go that way." He pointed left. "If you see her, don't approach her. Just call me. I'll alert mall security and see if we can nab her before she hits one of the exits."

Bridget searched for forty minutes and more, without success. She couldn't believe they had come this close only to lose her. Hopefully Nick would have better luck. But though she kept her phone close to hand, it never rang.

An hour later, she returned, defeated, to the bookstore. She was disappointed to find Nick waiting, his expression glum.

"Damn. We were so close," he groaned.

"Are you sure it was her?" But though she'd never met the girl in person, Bridget knew it had been.

Nick swore again. "We had all the exits monitored within five minutes. She must have made it out of the mall quickly."

"Or else she's found a good hiding spot."

"If that's the case, she'll be found, eventually. I called in some of our guys who were in the vicinity. Between them and mall security they'll be giving this place a clean sweep."

"We can stay longer and help."

"I'd like to, but I promised Matt I'd pick up Mandy half an hour ago."

"I could do that for you."

"Thanks, but that's okay. We're checking just to be cautious, but I'm positive Tara is long gone. I tried running from here to the closest exit and it only took me ninety seconds."

Later, in the car, en route to Matt and Jane's house, Bridget realized there was a silver lining to what they'd seen. "At least we know she's alive and well. And she isn't being help captive somewhere."

"That's true," Nick agreed. "Was it my imagination or was there a moment when she considered turning herself in?"

"I had a similar impression. That girl is in over her head, Nick. I only wish she could have trusted us to help her."

MANDY WAS TIRED and cried off and on during the drive home from Matt and Jane's house. Nick could feel the tension ratcheting in his neck as each minute passed. He hated listening to his daughter's distress and not being able to do anything about it.

If they hadn't seen Tara Lang in the mall, he would have been able to pick Mandy up earlier, before she became so overtired.

Finally he pulled onto their street. Bridget offered to help him get Mandy settled and he was only too glad to accept.

Mandy's blubbering stopped as soon as she was in his arms. She sighed and her body relaxed against him.

"I'll prepare her milk," Bridget offered, following him inside. "You go ahead and change Mandy."

"Thanks." He carried his daughter to the room that had become hers. He stripped off Mandy's outfit, removed her wet cloth diaper and tossed it into the container with the other soiled diapers.

By the time Mandy was dressed in her sleepers, Bridget had a bottle of milk warmed and ready.

Fifteen minutes later, Mandy was fed, dry and cozy in her crib.

"She looks so peaceful," Bridget said.

They were standing side by side, staring down at the sleeping baby. Nick noticed Bridget's hand on the rail of the crib, so small and feminine next to his.

"Thanks for staying and helping." Looking after babies was much easier with two.

Lots of things were easier…not to mention more fun…with two.

As Bridget bent to give a gentle kiss to Mandy's

cheek, he caught a hint of her fragrance. Her long, wild hair brushed his arm. The vee of her sweater dipped low enough for him to see the curve of her breasts, so sweetly generous.

Nick was tired after the long day at work, Christmas shopping at the mall, the futile search for Tara Lang, and the rush to get Mandy into bed.

He ought to feel exhausted, hungry and grumpy.

But he felt alive, aware, alert. Every nerve in his body was craving something right now and it wasn't sleep or food.

He couldn't believe there had ever been a time when he hadn't thought Bridget was attractive. The packaging was unusual—today Bridget had on jeans decorated with embroidered flowers, colorful socks, a bright pink sweater. She would never belong on a model's runway.

But the woman inside the clothes was adorable and feminine and hot.

CHAPTER THIRTEEN

"BABIES ARE SO MUCH WORK," Bridget said, still looking at Mandy. "But the rewards are amazing."

Suddenly Nick felt guilty for wanting her. Bridget wasn't into wild, impetuous affairs. She chose her guys carefully—stable and solid guys like Matt and Gavin.

Why would she take a risk on someone with his track record? And why would he want to mess up what was turning out to be a great friendship? He liked having Bridget in his life. Even once Mandy was back home with her mother, he didn't want that to change.

"It's been a crazy evening. How about a beer? I have a frozen pizza, too, if you're hungry."

"I am," she said, as if surprised by the fact.

They went to the kitchen and he handed Bridget two bottles of ale and the opener, so he could preheat the oven and get the pizza out of the wrapping.

"Thanks for asking me to help you with your daughter, Nick. The past few days have been wonderful. It's really made me think about my future and what I want."

"And that future…let me guess…would it include babies?" he teased.

Her expression grew dreamy. "Maybe. I hope. A family can't always be planned. A lot of things would need to change in my life for that to happen."

Like…she would have to meet the right man. Nick swallowed, thinking the guy she chose was going to be damn lucky.

"You'll make an excellent mother, Bridge."

"Do you really think so?"

"No doubt about it."

She smiled, and it was beautiful. Genuine and warm.

She touched his arm impulsively. "You're already a great dad, Nick. You're so lucky to have a daughter like Mandy."

He did feel lucky. But he couldn't agree that he was much good as a father. He always felt he was flying by the seat of his pants. He wasn't a natural like his brothers.

They sat at the table with their bottles of beer. Most women would have asked for a glass for their beer. He wondered if any of them knew how erotic it was to see a woman drinking straight from the bottle. The way Bridget was doing now.

He couldn't take his eyes off her plump, juicy lips pressed to the glass. Then she tipped her head back and he saw the tender, white skin of her neck, leading to the vee of her sweater, the swell of her breasts.

He forced his eyes away, to the cool bottle in his hand, and thought about how easy it was to underestimate someone. He'd seen Bridget around the neigh-

C. J. CARMICHAEL   149

borhood for years. The fact that she dressed a little differently and looked after dogs had caused him to pigeonhole her.

Never had he looked deeply enough to see her true beauty. Never would he have guessed that she'd studied physics in university. Was a Harvard grad.

"How did you end up doing what you're doing? I mean, you didn't just abandon physics to piss off your parents, did you?"

"No. I tried a career in science for a few years. But I discovered I don't like spending my days in labs or offices. I like being out-of-doors and having some control over my schedule."

"So that explains the dog-sitting."

She nodded. "I didn't want to look after a big kennelful of dogs, so I decided to offer an exclusive service to pet owners who could afford to have their dogs pampered a little."

"What about the numerology stuff? I still can't understand how that jibes with your scientific training."

"Better than you might think. I've always wanted to believe that there is order in the chaos. To me random coincidence can't explain the magic that I see in life every day."

"Isn't that the purpose of science? To explain how our world works?"

"But there's so much it can't explain. For me numerology is an attempt to fill in the gap. And while I can't prove why it seems to work, the fact that my clients find it helpful, and I find it helpful, is enough for me."

She was passionate about what she believed in. He'd give her that.

"Tell me your birth date, Nick."

Instinctively he recoiled.

"Come on. What can it hurt? Let me guess the year…1975?"

"'74." Maybe if he played along, she'd finally give him some peace.

"Do you have a piece of paper?"

He rolled his eyes, then handed her the pad and pen he kept by the phone.

"Okay, so you add all the digits of your year of birth like this—one plus nine plus seven plus four equals twenty-one. But we need to reduce to a single digit, so we take it one step further like this—two plus one equals three. That's your birth year number. Now, what date were you born on?"

He sighed with resignation. She'd gone this far, he didn't suppose he could stop her now. "June seven."

"Okay, so June is the sixth month, which means your birth month is six. And your birth date is seven. So now we add the year, month and date—three plus six plus seven equals sixteen. And one step further…one plus six equals seven." She smiled smugly. "I thought so."

"You thought so. What the hell does that mean?"

"It explains why you became a detective. Sevens are analytical and inquisitive. But seven can also be a very isolating expression. Which explains why it's so difficult for you to form a long, stable relationship with a woman."

"Oh, really?" He wanted like hell to challenge that judgment. But, damn it, his history would only prove her point. If it hadn't, he might have kissed her then. A guy could only resist so much, for so long.

But then the buzzer sounded for the pizza. And food was sometimes the safest substitute for sex.

BRIDGET WENT HOME as soon as they finished their pizza and beer. Nick was about to hit the sack when his home phone rang. It was Jessica, calling from Australia.

"Hey, Nick. How are you and Mandy?"

"If you'd called a few days ago, I would be freaking right now. But we're figuring things out."

"Is she eating okay?"

"Sure. The sitter I hired is making her all this mashed organic goop that she really likes."

"What's the sitter like? Did you check her references?"

"Didn't need to. Bridget lives two doors down. I've known her for years. She's great with Mandy."

"Well. Good for you. I knew you'd be able to handle this."

"It's nice to know you have so much confidence in me."

"Why not? Nick, you never fail at anything."

He was surprised to hear her say that. "What about our divorce? I consider that a pretty damn big failure."

There was a long pause. He wondered if she'd hung up.

"That's not fair. Not to you or to me. The thing we

did wrong wasn't the divorce. It was getting married in the first place."

He couldn't buy that. "You don't think Mandy was worth it?"

"How does Mandy benefit if two people, who don't love each other, get married and try to live together?"

"You don't think people can grow to love each other?"

"That was the argument you used to convince me to marry you. And I fell for it. But if I was in the same situation ever again, I wouldn't. Love can't grow without a solid foundation and you and I didn't have that. We'd had some fun dates, some very good sex. That's all."

He heard a male voice in the background.

"Look, I've got to go. I'll call again in a couple of days. Give Mandy a kiss for me, okay?"

"But—"

She hung up before he had a chance to ask her about Mandy's nocturnal wakings. He turned off the phone, then sank onto his mattress, staring up at the ceiling.

Some fun dates. Some very good sex. Was that all he was capable of when it came to relationships with the opposite sex? Jessica seemed to think so.

Possibly there was more to this numerology stuff than he wanted to admit.

THE ATMOSPHERE at the station was tense on Wednesday morning. Nick's mood wasn't improved by the fact that Mandy had woken again, twice, during the night.

He rounded a corner and almost bumped into one of his fellow officers with a grim expression and a sheet of paper in her hand. She seemed to be in a hurry.

"What's up, Jenn?"

"You haven't seen the morning paper." It wasn't a question but an observation and she didn't stop to elaborate. "Excuse me, but I've got to get this fax out right now."

His own pace quickened as he made his way along the corridor. In the briefing room, Glenn had a chair saved for him. As Nick slid into his seat, he noticed the unmistakable stench of alcohol seeping from his partner's pores. Glenn's eyes were bloodshot, but still he had the balls to wink.

"You okay?" Nick asked.

"Rough night. But I'm all right now."

Nick wasn't so sure his partner would pass a Breathalyzer test. He got up to snag a couple of coffees and passed one to Glenn. At the front of the room, the Chief of Detectives was preparing to speak.

"Any idea what was in the newspaper today?" Nick asked quietly.

Glenn had folded the front page in half. He passed it over. The bold lettering at the top read: Attorney General's Daughter Missing. A caption lower down the page posed the question, "Did she run away or was she abducted?"

The editors had a copy of the very picture Nick had in his jacket pocket. Tara Lang's young face stared belligerently from under the headline.

Nick swore. Well, the shit had hit the fan. He

wasn't too surprised. Tara had been missing for over a week and they'd interviewed a lot of people. It was inevitable that word would reach the press. Maybe the lifeguard at the pool had a friend who worked for the paper. Or perhaps the link had come from one of the kids at school.

The source of the leak was beside the point, anyway. The crucial fact here was that the public now knew Vincent Lang's daughter was missing. This was bound to affect their investigation. Tactically, the leak might be a good thing.

Politically, it was a nightmare.

Chief Wilson raised his hand. The room grew silent.

"This wasn't supposed to happen." He held up a copy of the paper. "I don't need to tell you that certain people are going to be very unhappy that it did." He paused. "But I'm not one of them."

The mood in the room immediately brightened. Officers around Nick let out their breath, relaxed their shoulders. Tight lips curved into smiles.

"What are you all looking so damned happy about?" The Chief's words came out like the bark of an angry dog. "If we'd done our jobs properly there would be no need for a headline like this today. Tara Lang would be safely asleep at her home with her parents."

With that admonishment, the Chief launched into a lecture, and from there, an action plan. The word was out, the public had been alerted. If Tara Lang was on the street somewhere, she was bound to be spotted today.

NICK SPENT the day going over old ground. He didn't know what else to do. In the office a detective was fielding tips from the public. But so far none of the calls had turned up anything new.

Glenn seemed content to ride along in the car with him. He kept complaining about the sunshine, popping painkillers for his headache. Nick, on the other hand, was glad it wasn't snowing for a change. He kept pushing water and coffee at his partner, trying to dilute Glenn's blood-alcohol levels.

Every now and then Glenn went on a bender like this. Not usually on a weekday, though. Nick sent his partner several worried looks on the ride to the mall. Finally Glenn exploded on him.

"Cut it out with the mother hen act, okay? I went overboard last night, but I've got it back under control."

"Well, make sure that you do."

Glenn just grunted in reply.

Nick parked at the mall then he and Glenn patrolled through the corridors, stopping at the food court for a sandwich for lunch. Glenn took a few bites of his, then lost interest.

"Are you okay?"

Nick expected Glenn to brush off his concern again, but surprisingly, he gave a serious answer.

"I don't usually go on a tear when I'm working. Last night was tough. An ex-girlfriend was in town. She looked me up."

"Yeah? And were you glad to see her?"

"I thought I was. Shaved and put on a clean

sweater. Met her for coffee downtown and she looked damn good."

"Sounds like your lucky night."

"Hardly. She had pictures of her husband and two kids. Said she was in town for a convention and wanted to thank me for breaking up with her. She never would have had such a terrific life if she'd stayed with me."

"God. That was brutal. Good for her she's made a nice life for herself. But why rub it in your face?"

"I guess I treated her kind of crappy way back when."

"Oh." Nick didn't know what else to say. A perverse part of his mind had him imagining himself twenty years from now, meeting up with Bridget in the same way.

Thanks for not sleeping with me, Nick. I've had a great life without you.

A cute salesclerk walked by, wearing a Santa hat and a red sweater. Nick's thoughts turned to Christmas. "What are you doing for the holidays?"

"Not much. My mom passed away last year and my brother and his family live on the West Coast."

"You could fly over for a visit."

"Airports are crazy this time of year."

Nick didn't think Christmas was such a big deal either. But he couldn't imagine it without his daughter and his mother and brothers. For some reason Bridget's silly Christmas tree came to mind. And the sweet and spicy smell of her house when she'd been baking.

"Might be worth the hassle," Nick said. "To be with family."

Glenn shook his head. "Don't have any. This is my life, man." He winked at the cute girl, standing in line for a taco.

The girl didn't seem to notice.

Glenn shrugged. "Never hurts to try." He stood up. "Finished?"

They dumped their trash in the bins, then headed for the nearest exit. Nick felt a bit depressed, on his partner's behalf, but Glenn whistled lightly as they made their way to the car.

Once they were back on the road, Nick checked in with the dispatcher, who had nothing new to offer him.

They drove past Tara's school and watched as the kids were let out at three o'clock. Nick hoped Tara might be hiding somewhere nearby…but they saw no sign of her. At quarter past three, he told his partner about his plan to visit Colin Porter's house.

"The English teacher? What's the point of that? We've talked to him twice now. You really think he has anything new to tell you?"

"It's just a feeling I have. I'd like to interview him away from the school. He might be more relaxed."

Glenn shrugged. "Fine, but drop me off at the station first. I've got hours of reports to catch up on."

It was almost four when Nick drove up to Colin Porter's apartment building, about two miles from the school. The modest dwelling, three stories with four units on each level, was certainly within the means of a man earning a teacher's salary.

Nick parked and took quick reconnaissance of the neighborhood. Nothing out of the ordinary. He approached the building slowly, counted up the floors until he'd figured out which unit was Porter's. The curtains on the side and front windows were all drawn. That seemed weird for this time of day.

He rang the manager's bell, provided identification and was granted access to the building. He stood outside the door for unit ten for a moment, certain he could hear something—voices, or maybe a television—from inside. But when he knocked on the door a full minute passed with no response.

He knocked again. "Police. I'd like to have a few words."

Whether his voice had carried or not, he wasn't sure. But suddenly Colin Porter was there, opening the door.

"Detective? This is a surprise."

CHAPTER FOURTEEN

NICK FIXED his gaze on Colin Porter. It was a stare meant to scare the truth out of your average law-abiding citizen. But either Porter wasn't average or he wasn't law-abiding, because he didn't quake.

"Has there been bad news?" Porter pinched the bridge of his slender nose, as if preparing himself.

"About Tara? No." Not yet, anyway. "May I come in?"

"Of course."

Beyond the small entranceway was the living room, with a big-screen TV, turned off, and a sectional sofa. The cushions had indents as if someone had been lying on them recently. A blanket was pooled on the floor. On the coffee table were a half-eaten bag of chips and a diet-cola can.

"It's dark in here," he commented.

"The sunlight fades the furniture." Even as Porter said this, he was pulling back the curtains, admitting the weak afternoon light.

Straight ahead a corridor led to the kitchen. The place was so silent, Nick could hear a tap dripping from the sink. "Someone here with you, Mr. Porter?"

"No. I live alone."

But Nick had heard voices, and neither the TV nor the radio were on. Perhaps Porter had just switched them off.

"If you read the morning paper, I guess you know Tara Lang is still missing."

"I did see that, yes."

"I have some follow-up questions, but would you mind if I had a drink of water, first?"

Had he imagined the flash of annoyance on Porter's face? A moment later Colin Porter was impeccably polite as he invited Nick to follow him to the kitchen.

"Would you like ice?"

"No, thanks." Nick surveyed the room. He saw a plate littered with crumbs on the counter. Another cola can, not diet this time. A knife that looked as if it had been used to spread peanut butter. "Do you like smooth or crunchy, Mr. Porter?"

"Pardon me?"

"Peanut butter. Which kind do you prefer?"

At that moment, Porter noticed the knife, too. He handed Nick his water, then picked up the knife and placed it in the dishwasher. "Smooth," he said.

"I like crunchy." He drank some of the water, then glanced down the hall to his left toward the bedrooms. Two doors were open, but he couldn't see inside. The third door was closed.

"Nice place," he said. "I live in a townhome. Not much yard, but still it's a pain. Must be nice not to worry about mowing the lawn."

"An apartment suits me fine, since I like to travel in the summer."

"What about over the Christmas holidays? Got any plans?"

"Not really." He glanced at his watch. "I was hoping to catch an early movie. You said you had questions?"

The longer he prolonged his visit, the more uncomfortable Porter seemed to get. Nick took his time removing his notebook from his jacket pocket.

"My partner and I were just exploring a new angle in the case," he said. "And I wondered if any of Tara's essays might have shown an unhealthy interest in older men."

Porter's eyes flickered, but he showed no other reaction. "No."

"Wouldn't you like to review her work before you give such a definitive answer?"

"I return all my students' essays to them after I've finished marking. But I have no problem recalling the content of Tara's English assignments. There was nothing in them of the nature you described." He cleared his throat. "This new avenue of investigation…do you have any specific suspicions?"

"I'm not at liberty to say."

Nick took another drink of water. He wasn't surprised that Porter hadn't invited him to sit. Although the teacher's posture, as he leaned into the kitchen counter, appeared casual, the man was vibrating with tension.

"Mind if I use the facilities?" He glanced casually down the hallway, starting to move in that direction.

Porter stepped in front of him. "Sorry. I have a blockage problem at the moment."

"Really." Nick drilled the guy with a stare, but Porter didn't flinch.

"Sorry for the inconvenience," he added.

Right. As Nick backed off, he noticed a laptop computer in an alcove next to the fridge. The screen showed a display for a car rental agency. "Are you sure you're not planning a trip, Mr. Porter?"

"It's not definite. I'm just considering the idea." Casually, Porter moved to the computer and closed the lid. Noticing Nick was finished his water, he reached for the glass. "Is that all, then?"

Nick glanced again at the shut door down the hall. Then at the computer. "Yes, that's all, Mr. Porter." He went to the front door where he slipped on his boots. "Enjoy your movie."

Nick took his time walking to the car. As he settled into the driver's seat, he noticed the front drapes being pulled closed again. He sat and watched a long while. No one left or entered the apartment building for half an hour. If Colin Porter really was planning to go to a movie, he was going to be very late.

BRIDGET'S INSTINCTS about Colin Porter had been dead on. How had she known?

Nick drove straight from Porter's place to Bridget's. When he rang the bell, Bridget called for him to come in. She was feeding Mandy in the kitchen and the sight of the two of them was incredibly calming. The tension in his gut eased and he managed to smile. Green mush rimmed Mandy's mouth as she smiled at him.

"Hey there, sweetie." She really was the cutest thing. "Are you enjoying your dinner?"

"She sure is. Want to take over?"

"You bet." He deliberately let his fingers touch Bridget's as she passed him the spoon. Their eyes met.

Bridget was wearing purple. A flowing top over jeans and a matching headband. The color made her skin seem pale and creamy. The green of her eyes jumped out at him.

Today her eyes made him think of a witch. Maybe because he was still spooked at how she'd picked the English teacher's name from out of that list.

"I went to see Colin Porter today."

"Oh?" She moved her hand away, stepping back a few feet.

"It was a very interesting visit." He turned his attention to his daughter, filling the spoon with some of the rice and green bean puree. "Here comes the police cruiser, Mandy…."

Bridget rolled her eyes at him. "You are sooo corny." But she couldn't completely hide her smile. She gathered Mandy's blanket and clean bottle and packed them into the pink diaper bag.

"Tara's disappearance made the papers today," he said. "Apparently Vincent Lang is livid."

"Yes, I read the story. Do you know who leaked it?"

It sounded like an innocent question, but something about Bridget's expression tipped him off. "We don't. Do you?"

"How could I know?"

"I have no idea. Just like I have no idea how you picked Colin Porter's name out of that list I gave you."

"You know how. You just don't want to admit it."

He knew she wanted him to validate her belief in numerology. But he didn't answer. Just spooned more food into Mandy's mouth.

Bridget sighed. "Fine. We won't talk about that."

"Thank you."

"Will you tell me what happened when you went to Colin's house? What did you find?"

"Nothing major. Just lots of little things that didn't feel right."

"Such as?"

"Do you mind turning on the TV while I tell you? It's almost six and I'd like to see the news."

"Sure." She went to the living room and a few seconds later he heard a familiar broadcaster's voice discussing world events. Local news wouldn't be on for a while yet.

When Bridget returned, she perched on the counter and looked at him expectantly.

"Colin Porter lives in an apartment," he told her. "And the first strange thing I noticed was that he had his curtains drawn. The only sunny day we've had in a week and he blocks it out? He claimed he was worried about the sunlight fading the furniture, but what guy cares about stuff like that?"

"Not many would," she agreed.

"Then there were the cola cans. Diet in the living room. Regular in the kitchen."

"Most people drink one or the other. So he had a visitor."

"Yeah. Only he'd just gotten home from work. So where was there time for someone to pop by?"

"Unless someone was staying in the apartment while he was at the school."

Nick nodded. "There was a half-eaten bag of chips in the living room. And a knife with peanut butter in the kitchen."

"The kind of food a teenager would like."

"Yeah." Nick scraped up the rest of Mandy's dinner and fed her the last spoonful. Then he wiped her mouth and passed her the clean spoon to play with.

"Do you think he's hiding her? Were you able to look for her?"

"I could only go as far as I was invited. Porter made up an excuse when I asked to use his washroom. I couldn't do more without a search warrant. And, unfortunately, I'll need hard evidence to get a judge to give me one of those."

"Oh, Nick, do you really think she's there? Could he be holding her against her will?"

"I doubt it. We saw her in the mall just yesterday. If she had that much freedom, she could have returned home. Or when she realized I was a cop, she could have asked for help."

"Maybe she thinks she's in love with him. But she's only fourteen and…oh, God. I hope he isn't…"

She didn't finish. Didn't need to.

"Whatever's going on, it's sick," Nick agreed. "And I'm afraid we're running out of time to extricate Tara from the situation. Porter's home computer was open to the Web page of a car-rental agency. My guess is that as soon as school lets out on Friday, he and Tara will leave Hartford. Most likely he'll want to drive her across the state line, head to some isolated countryside and…"

He stopped. No need to mention the possibilities. They were all too obvious.

"I'm so worried about her, Nick. She's naive and idealistic…the perfect victim for someone like Porter."

"I'm afraid so."

"How do you think this started?"

"My guess is that after her fight with her parents on Tuesday night, Tara turned to the one person she knew would be sympathetic—her English teacher. Colin must have been patiently laying the groundwork all semester. Singling her out for attention in the classroom. Giving her high grades and praising the one thing that mattered most to her…her poetry. When Tara came crying, he was perfectly positioned to play the part of the protector and offer her a place to stay."

"Meanwhile, Tara's too innocent and self-centered to question what his true motives might be. Oh, Nick. Maybe you should break into Colin's place tomorrow while he's at school."

"I'd love to," he admitted. "But what if Tara isn't there, or she's there but doesn't want to be found? I break into that apartment without just cause and I'm in deep trouble."

"We can't let him take her away."

"Of course not." A phrase on the television caught his attention and he paused to listen.

"And now for the latest on the District Attorney's daughter…"

He picked up Mandy and headed for the living room. Bridget followed with the remote control, turning up the volume.

Tara's picture was on the television screen. The announcer was mid-sentence into her report: "…missing since Tuesday night or possibly Wednesday morning. And now we go to the distraught parents. Mr. Lang, how are you and Mrs. Lang coping with this terrible situation?"

The camera zeroed in on Tara's parents. As her father murmured bullshit about being worried and hoping his baby girl was safe, Nick read the real story on his face. He was pissed off as hell.

Then it was Tara's mother's turn on camera. Annabel looked *old*. Her eyes were tearing and puffy. She'd outlined her lips with color, but some of it had leached into the fine lines around her mouth.

"If anyone knows where my daughter is…I beg you, come forward." Annabel swallowed. "Or, Tara, if you're watching…honey, please…."

And then she stopped. She couldn't say anything more. The camera zoomed back to the reporter, who wrapped up the story with a plea to the public to phone the police with any news.

When the broadcast moved to the next story, Bridget flicked off the set. Her eyes were filled with tears, and Nick remembered that this was personal for her. She *knew* these people.

"Annabel is a good person," Bridget said softly. "She is a good mother, too. She doesn't deserve any of this."

He noticed she didn't say anything about Vincent.

"Nick, we have to tell her where her daughter is."

"We don't know where Tara is," he reminded her. "We *think* we know based on hunches, intuitions and…numerology. That's all we've got. What we need is evidence. Fact."

"So Colin Porter wins. Is that what you're telling me?"

"No. If I'm right and Porter is planning to take Tara out of state, at some point he'll have to move her from the building to the car. I just have to be waiting when he does."

"You can't watch his apartment twenty-four hours a day."

"I don't plan to. I think we can count on the fact that Porter doesn't want to draw any attention to himself. That means that he has to keep showing up at work until school lets out for the holidays. We won't have to worry about him skipping town until the Christmas break. Starting Friday after school, I'll keep surveillance on his apartment." Nick set his mouth in a stubborn line. "I'm going to stop him, Bridge. I can't let him hurt that girl."

"I only hope he hasn't hurt her already."

Nick said nothing to that. He simply held his daughter a little bit tighter.

ON THURSDAY MORNING, Nick felt half-dead as he made his way to work, arriving early despite his exhaustion. He grabbed a coffee, wishing he didn't have to go to the work of drinking it, but could just inject the caffeine straight into his system.

Lack of sleep was one of his problems. But he was also feeling frustrated and powerless about the Tara Lang case.

And then there was Bridget. He'd caught her in her housecoat this morning when he'd dropped off Mandy. Who would have guessed such a down-to-earth woman would wear silk to bed? When she'd reached for Mandy, he'd seen the full outline of her breasts, including pert nipples.

He'd longed to grab her and haul her into the bedroom right then and there.

Good God, his life was a mess.

Nick rounded the corridor, then headed to Captain Harper's office. No more thinking about Bridget. He needed to focus for this conversation with his boss.

"Gray. Come in." The Captain looked just about as rough as Nick felt. "We've had no breaks over the night. Tell me you've come up with something."

"I've got a theory. That's about it. I'm thinking she might be holed up with her English teacher, Colin Porter."

"That's a stretch. On what evidence?"

"None." Nick would rather have shown up to work in a tutu and dancing slippers than mention a word about numerology. "It's just a gut feeling I have about the man."

The Captain had some respect for that. At the same time, he had limited resources. Putting a tail on Porter twenty-four seven just couldn't happen. But he agreed with the action plan Nick laid out before him.

Nick left the meeting ten minutes later to hunt for his partner. He found Glenn plowing through old e-mails on Tara's hard drive. His partner was in better shape this morning. But when he got closer, Nick caught a whiff of stale alcohol.

"I went back about six months and look what I found." Glenn passed him a series of messages he'd printed out and stapled into a package. Certain key words and dates had been highlighted in yellow.

Nick flipped through the printouts. The e-mails were from a guy who called himself songbird121. He claimed to be fifteen years old and interested in songwriting.

"Tara writes him about lyrics and poetry and stuff and while he claims to love that shit, too, he keeps trying to set up a meeting with her," Glenn said.

"Yeah?" Intrigued, Nick flipped to the last of the messages. "Did she ever meet the guy?"

"No. She kept putting him off."

"Smart girl."

"Maybe. Or maybe after she had that fight with her parents, she decided to give songbird another

chance? She had his phone number." Glenn pointed
to a highlighted number on one of the e-mails.

"We ought to check that out," Nick admitted. He'd
come in all fired up about Colin Porter. But he
couldn't close his mind to other possibilities.

"I'm on it." Ten minutes later Glenn had set up an
appointment with a man named Gilbert Olsen. "He
sounded like he was in his forties, at least," Glenn
said after disconnecting the call.

Nick's stomach turned. "God, that's sick."

Glenn grabbed his coat. "I'll handle this. Let me
know how things pan out with Colin Porter."

Nick nodded, on the way out the door himself.
Today he planned to knock on doors in Porter's neighborhood. It was winter and most people would be
sticking close to home. But maybe one of Porter's
neighbors had noticed a fourteen-year-old girl coming
and going. It was worth checking out, anyway.

Three hours later, Nick was feeling pretty discouraged. He'd been through the apartment building and
up and down the block and had found only four
neighbors home. None of them had seen anything
helpful. Apparently neighbors around here stuck to
themselves. Only one of them had been able to pick
Colin Porter's face from the school yearbook Nick
had brought along with him.

Nick headed slowly back to his car. He stopped and
looked up at Porter's unit. The curtains were drawn
again, even though clouds had been forecast for the
day. He circled the building, then, getting the superin-
tendent to let him inside, he went upstairs and pressed

an ear at Porter's door. At the smallest sound of distress, he would have stormed the front door. But all he could hear was the soft murmur of a television set.

He had a strong hunch Tara Lang was watching it. But what if she wasn't? What if Colin had just forgotten to turn it off before he left for work that morning?

He needed more justification than that to break in. Unfortunately.

Deciding he might as well stop for lunch, Nick returned to his car, intending to stop at the first burger place he found. He was just pulling onto the street when a call came through from his brother Matt.

"I have a client meeting in the old neighborhood this afternoon. Want to meet me at the Corner Diner for lunch?"

He needed a break from this god-awful day. And a visit with Matthew, combined with his favorite burger and shake, seemed just the ticket. "You bet. I can make it in ten minutes."

He picked up his speed, then headed toward the Hartford neighborhood where he and his brothers had grown up. The Corner Diner had been around for decades and he frequented the place often enough that he still knew most of the employees.

"Hi, Cindy," he said to the pretty young waitress who came to take his order once he was seated. "I'll have a coffee for now. I'm waiting for my brother."

"You're sure that's all you want, Nick?"

Cindy was used to him flirting with her. But today he wasn't in the mood. He gave her a tired smile.

"My six-month-old daughter was up twice last night. I didn't get much sleep. Trust me, coffee is exactly what I need right now."

Her eyes widened at the mention of his daughter, but she didn't say anything, just headed straight to the kitchen. Once upon a time he would have appreciated the swaying of her bottom in her low-rise jeans, but today he still had a silky nightgown and a wholesome smile on his mind. A minute later Cindy returned with his coffee, setting it on the table with a decisive thud.

His brother arrived then, dressed smartly, hair perfectly styled, not disheveled the way Nick's always seemed to be. God, older brothers could be such a pain.

Matthew tapped a fist to Nick's shoulder, then sat across from him. "You're looking a little rough, bro. Bad night?"

"Mandy's still not sleeping through."

Matthew nodded. "That can be tough."

"I wish I knew what I was doing wrong."

"These things just take time."

Cindy returned to the table to take their orders. When she left, Matthew raised an eyebrow. In the past he had teased Nick about his penchant for flirting with the waitstaff. Undoubtedly he'd noticed the cool interplay between them today.

"Did you piss her off?"

Nick shrugged.

"Cripes, you really have changed, haven't you?"

"I'm tired and I'm working on an important case

right now. Excuse me if I don't have the energy to smile at a pretty woman."

"Does the new dog-sitter have something to do with your lack of interest in other women? Not to mention your foul mood, which, come to think of it, might be caused by sexual frustration. You haven't had much previous experience with that, have you, Nick?"

CHAPTER FIFTEEN

HIS OLDEST BROTHER had always enjoyed pressing his hot button. "You want me to pop you one on the nose?" Nick asked. "Why the hell are you pushing me like this?"

"That's what big brothers are for. And now I remember her name. It's Bridget, right? Why don't you just ask her out?" Matt asked.

"Ha. That shows what you know."

"It is common procedure when you're attracted to a woman."

"That's just it. I'm not."

Matt shook his head. "Huh? You're bent out of shape about a woman you're not attracted to?"

"I wasn't in the beginning. I am now. The problem is, I like her, okay? I really like her. She lives two doors down from me and I want her to keep liking me, too."

"Maybe she already does. More than you think."

"She's into long-term, steady guys. And she knows too much about my track record with women."

"The divorce still eating at you?"

"What would you know about it?"

"Hey. I've been there, remember?" Matt splayed his hand on the table. His new wedding ring sparkled in the afternoon light, but Nick could remember a time when his brother had worn a different gold ring. He closed his eyes and rubbed his fingers across his forehead.

Why was he arguing with Matt, when what he really wanted was some advice?

"Sometimes I forget what you've been through," he admitted. "I think of you and Gavin being so perfect and I'm always the screwup."

"When it comes to women, we're all vulnerable, Nick. Not one of us managed to get it right the first time. I'm not sure why, but it is what it is. The important thing is to learn from your mistakes. For you, Jessica was a mistake. Maybe this Bridget isn't."

"You don't think it would be wrong of me to ask her out? Given my less-than-stellar track record with women?"

"It depends on your motives. If you honestly like her. If you see potential for something bigger, something that might last forever, well, Nick, how can you not give it a shot?"

WAS MATT RIGHT? Should he take a shot with Bridget and just hope things worked out? The idea was tempting and frightening all at the same time.

After lunch Nick went back to headquarters and spent the next couple of hours calling car-rental agencies in Hartford, hoping to find a booking by Colin Porter.

He came up with nothing. Which left three possibilities.

He was wrong and Colin Porter had no plans to travel over Christmas.

He'd scared Porter off and so he hadn't yet booked the car.

Or—and this seemed most likely to Nick—Porter had used a fake ID to make the reservation. Which made him a much craftier and sophisticated adversary than Nick had imagined.

He was frowning over his second cup of coffee that afternoon, when he received a call from Annabel Lang.

"Detective Gray?"

She sounded upset. "Yes?"

"I hate to be a bo-bother…" She choked back a sob. "B-but I was hoping you could drop by the house. I need to talk to you."

"Give me twenty-five minutes."

He ended up arriving in fifteen. Patting his jacket to make sure he had his notebook, he jogged up the walk. Just like the last time he'd visited the estate home, the front door opened before he'd announced his presence.

Annabel Lang was dressed in baggy sweatpants and a bulky sweater. Her eyes were red, her hair pulled back in a simple ponytail.

Now *this* was the mother he'd expected to see at the start of the investigation.

"Detective. Thank you so much for coming. Let's go to my office."

She led him to a different room this time. It was

obviously a woman's retreat, with white furniture, a sleek glass desk and modern cabinetry. On the desk was a slender vase with a single white rose.

Annabel fingered the petals gently, then turned to face him. "Where is she, Detective?"

It was an anguished plea from a distraught mother, and Nick felt the burden of having to admit he didn't know. She'd been updated earlier about the sighting at the mall. He reminded her of this now, and that at least they knew that two days ago Tara had been fine.

"Yes. But where did she go? And where is she now?"

He could have made an educated guess, of course, but it was much too soon to voice those suspicions.

"We are working full-time on this case, Mrs. Lang. We're covering all the bases." He knew his words meant nothing to her. She wanted them to find her daughter. Until that happened, she would not be appeased.

"I thought you said it would make a difference if we went to the media. Well, my husband and I were all over the news last night. Did it help?"

"We've been fielding a lot of calls at the station. We check each tip carefully. Hopefully one of them will lead us to Tara soon, Mrs. Lang."

"What do *you* think, Detective? Do you have a theory about what's going on?"

He hesitated then decided to go out on a limb. "I can't make any promises. But I'm working on something. If it pans out, I'll know before the end of the week."

"Do you—do you think she's okay?"

"Two days ago she was," he reminded her. "We have no reason to think that she isn't still fine. Please don't torture yourself by imagining the worst."

"Can you tell me more about this theory of yours?" she pleaded.

Nick couldn't share his suspicions about Porter with Tara's mother. But it couldn't hurt to dig a little deeper. Maybe Annabel knew more than she realized.

"I've been following up closely with the teachers," he said carefully. "I wonder if you've met them? If you have any impressions you'd be willing to share, I'd appreciate hearing them."

Annabel wrapped her arms around her body, almost as if she was trying to support herself. It was difficult for Nick not to offer the grieving woman a hug. He waited, patiently, for her to pull herself together.

"I met the teachers once, at parent-teacher interviews, midway through the first semester," she said finally.

Nick pulled out his notebook, hoping for something, even a tidbit, that might help. "Did your husband attend the interviews, too?"

"No. Tara and I always go to these things together. It's difficult for Vincent to get away from the demands of his office."

There was a defensive edge to her voice, and Nick tried to put her at her ease. "I'm sure you told your husband everything he needed to know. But let's focus on the teachers right now. Say…Colin Porter. Do you recall your discussion with him?"

Annabel frowned. "Actually, he was the one teacher I didn't book a consult with. Tara convinced me to skip that interview since she had an A in his class."

"Was it rare for Tara to get an A?"

"Very. It didn't used to be," Annabel added quickly. "When she was younger, Tara was an excellent student. But puberty…" She sighed.

"Right. It happens." Nick listened as Annabel discussed her impression of the other teachers, more out of courtesy than anything else. What Tara's mother had just said only confirmed his own suspicion that Porter had given Tara good marks in his class in an attempt to win her over and to create a bond between them.

A bond he had eventually exploited to his own advantage.

When Annabel had finished telling him everything she could remember about Tara's teachers, Nick thanked her for her help.

"I'll be in touch as soon as I have any news for you," he promised.

They were about to leave the room when he noticed a business card that had been placed on top of one of the magazines artfully displayed on the coffee table. Nick glanced down and read the name of a well-known local TV journalist.

When he looked at Annabel her face had gone pale.

"May I take this?" he asked, reaching for the card.

She swallowed. Then nodded. "I should have thrown that away."

He slipped the card inside his notebook, then placed both back into his jacket pocket.

"Don't worry," he said gently, his impression of her going up a notch. "I won't tell anyone."

COMING HOME to Bridget and Mandy was the highlight of Nick's emotionally grueling day. As he swept Mandy into his arms and exchanged a warm smile with Bridget over the top of the baby's head, he felt a twinge of sympathy for his partner. Glenn had never experienced the simple joy of a welcome like this one.

Nick listened as Bridget filled him in on the day's activities. There'd been the usual walk, some stories, baking and finally, a yoga session in the afternoon.

"Mandy gets a kick out of listening to my yoga tape and watching me go through the postures."

"Really?" He loved hearing about the minutia of his daughter's life. When Jessica returned, he had to make sure they didn't slip back into the same schedule as before. He wanted to be part of Mandy's life. Not just a three-hour appointment on Sunday afternoons.

"I think I'd like to see you go through your postures, too," he added, eyeing her curves in her tight fitting pants and top. "By the way, you should definitely wear that outfit more often."

"I have the same request about those jeans of yours."

Her comment surprised him. Delighted him. "Really?" He eased a little closer to her. "So you think I look hot, huh?"

Her cheeks turned pink. She put a hand on his chest and pushed a little. "Tell me about *your* day. Any news on Tara?"

"I had a call from Annabel today—" The sound of the kitchen buzzer interrupted him.

"Yes, she told me she planned to call. Hang on while I get something out of the oven."

He followed, lured by more than the delicious scent wafting from the kitchen. He watched as she pulled yet another batch of cookies out of the oven, eyeing her curves, the exposed inch of skin at the small of her back.

"When did Annabel call you?"

"This morning. She needed to consult me on a few things. Not to do with Tara. At least not directly."

He wished she would tell him more, but she didn't. "What are your plans for the rest of the night?" he finally asked. "Do you have any appointments?"

"No. My clients are busy with holiday plans. Business will be slow until the January rush. New Year's resolutions," she added, raising her eyebrows. "It's always a busy time."

He perched Mandy on his knee and chatted to her as Bridget fussed around the kitchen. She'd baked other goodies today. Every surface in the room was covered with something. Red and white cookies twisted to look like candy canes, a big bowl of Poppycock and chocolate fudge.

"What are you going to do with all this?"

"I'll take most of it to the local senior's center, make gift baskets for my clients…and eat the rest."

Noticing him eye the fudge, she said, "Go ahead and take whatever you want."

"My Mom used to make fudge for Christmas," he said as he popped a piece in his mouth. But he didn't remember it tasting *this* good. Mandy reached out her hand, too.

"Sorry, sweetie. Fudge is definitely not on your menu plan." Noticing a bowl of puffed wheat on the table he gave her some of that instead.

She seemed perfectly content with the bargain.

Poor thing.

Finally Bridget stopped her puttering. She selected a piece of fudge for herself. She took a bite and closed her eyes, obviously savoring the taste.

His body reacted with a definite nod of approval. He didn't give himself time to think. "Would you like to go to a movie tonight?"

As soon as the words were out, he felt like clubbing his head. He'd asked out dozens of women in his life. Why had he blurted that out so awkwardly?

And why couldn't he breathe as he waited for her answer?

Bridget waited until she'd cleared the fudge from her teeth to say, "to a movie theater, you mean?"

"Yes, of course."

"What about Mandy?"

Oh, hell. He wasn't used to dating as a single father. Why hadn't he thought to ask Matt if he could babysit? "Uh. You're right. How about I run out and rent something?"

Even as he made the offer, he was thinking, *No,*

no, no. This was all wrong. This was not supposed to be a casual evening between friends. It was supposed to be a date.

"That would be better," Bridget agreed. "That way I can get a couple of loads of washing done at the same time."

For Pete's sake. She was going to do laundry?

Bridget didn't seem to notice his consternation. "What about dinner? The kitchen is a mess with all this baking. We could order pizza."

Nick sighed. So much for romance. It wasn't in the cards for tonight. Still, he felt a bone-deep feeling of contentment settle over him. Maybe a simple night with a DVD and pizza was just what he needed to counter the stress of the day.

"Joey's?" He named his favorite local pizza joint, then pulled out his phone.

"Speed dial, again?" Bridget sounded amused.

"You bet. What would you like?"

"I'll have the three-cheese vegetarian."

"I usually go for Italian meatball." He thought about all that garlic. "Actually I'll have the vegetarian, too."

THERE WAS SOMETHING different about Nick tonight. He'd suggested they watch *L.A. Confidential,* and since she'd never seen it before, she'd agreed. The fast-paced police drama had kept her riveted.

But not so riveted she hadn't noticed Nick's restlessness. Halfway through the movie Mandy had fallen asleep and Nick had tucked her into the portable crib in the spare room. When he'd returned it had seemed to Bridget that he'd sat a little closer to her on the sofa.

He'd definitely flirted with her earlier, when he'd made that comment about her yoga outfit. Was it possible when he'd asked if she wanted to go to a movie he'd intended it to be a date?

Every now and then when she looked at him, she felt a little jolt. Lots of movie stars had charisma on the screen. But in person, Nick had them beat. Bridget knew he'd do anything in his power to save Tara Lang. And in her books that made him a real-life hero, to boot.

Bridget reached for the last slice of pizza. She could feel Nick watching her. Did he think she was a pig? She set it back down.

He was still watching.

She studied his eyes, trying to guess what he was thinking. He'd seemed so stressed earlier. Part of the problem was lack of sleep, she knew. And of course he was stressed about Tara. But it seemed to her something else was on his mind tonight.

"I've never met anyone with eyes like yours," he said. "They're always changing. Right now they remind me of a cat's eyes. You know how you can never tell what the damn animals are thinking?"

"I'm a dog person," she reminded him. "How many beers have you had tonight?"

"I'm not inebriated, if that's what you're wondering."

Maybe not. But there were three empty cans on

the table and she'd been drinking juice. "Perhaps you and Mandy should spend the night again. The sheets in the spare room are clean."

"If I spend the night, it won't be in the spare room."

Her insides quivered. She ignored the feeling. "My sofa was that comfortable?"

He reached over and tangled his fingers in her hair. Her scalp had never tingled so pleasurably before.

"Remember our kiss?"

Speech was impossible. She nodded.

"I can't get it out of my mind. I can't get *you* out of my mind."

His words hit her with a flash of heat. "Me, too," she admitted.

"Want to do something about it?" He moved closer, stopped playing with her hair and placed his hand on the side of her face.

"You mean you want to be friends with benefits?"

"If you say the word *friends* one more time tonight I may have to kill you and hide your body under all that Christmas baking of yours."

She swallowed. But the lump in her throat still threatened to choke her.

"I was thinking *lovers,* Bridge."

CHAPTER SIXTEEN

LOVERS.

As Nick leaned forward to kiss her, a warning sounded in Bridget's head. He wasn't starting this with the intent to hurt her. But that was what would happen. Nick's relationships were passionate. Of that she had no doubt.

But they were also transitory.

Witness his marriage.

Did she really want to have an affair with a man like that?

His lips touched hers, warm, and oh, so skillful. He remembered all the things she'd liked from last time. The deep, intense connection of lips and mouth and tongue.

Beneath his hands, her back felt slender and supple as he pulled her closer. She fell into him, loving the breadth of his chest and shoulders and the way he made her feel delicate and precious within his embrace.

He kissed her again, stroking her back, then running his hands round to her belly and under her top. She felt as if she were melting and burning, all at the same time.

"Let me take you to your bedroom," he whispered, his breath enticing in her ear.

She tensed. "But Mandy—"

"She's in the other room. We'll close the door." He laughed softly. "I think married couples do this all the time."

"I guess you would know."

"Not from personal experience. Jessica and I were separated before—damn. I don't want to talk about her. I want to make love to *you*."

Oh, Lord. She had no capacity to say no to him. So what if the affair didn't last forever. This was something she couldn't stop.

"Yes, Nick," she said.

He reached for her and led her to the bedroom. Bridget kept six pillows on her bed. Four decorative, two functional. Nick tossed them all to the floor, then turned back to her.

He kissed her again, burrowing his hands in her hair. She felt her headband sliding off, then her hair tumbling over her shoulders.

"Why are you always tying back this gorgeous hair?"

"It gets in the way."

He brushed it away from her face then removed his hands and let it cascade forward. "This hair makes you look wild and sexy, Bridge."

"I guess it has its uses."

"I'll say. But this doesn't." Nick pulled the hem of her top smoothly up and over her head. "Pretty bra." He slid a finger under the lace strap, released the catch and let it fall. His touch was so soft, so perfect for this first stage of seduction.

She slid her hands down his back, dipping her fingers under the waistband of his jeans. His back was smooth skin and hard muscle, and when he pulled off his T-shirt, she saw that his entire upper body had the same muscular bulk.

They helped each other out of the rest of their clothes, and then he picked her up as if she hardly weighed a thing. Laying her back on the bed, he leaned over her, his eyes dark and heavy lidded.

"Tell me what you want," he invited.

She could only wet her lips and stare at him. *You,* she thought. *I want you.*

"If you don't set any limits, I won't know where to stop," he warned. And then he started to kiss her. Not on her mouth this time, but along her collarbone, and then her breasts. Exquisite little nips and gentle swirls with his tongue.

Her back arched as he kissed lower. She tangled her fingers in his hair and gave a little tug. He kissed her everywhere, everywhere, and she felt the pleasure beginning to spiral.

"Nick, wait."

"I hate those words."

She laughed and pulled him up to lie beside her. "Let me kiss you, too." She needed to explore his body the way he'd explored hers. Pushing him back, she let her hair fall over his chest and his belly as she pressed kisses to his hot skin. Her hair and her kisses trailed lower and Nick moaned.

"Come here, you witch." He pulled her up and again she felt the raw power of his arms. "Red hair, green eyes. You were born to torment me, weren't you?"

SEVERAL HOURS LATER Bridget and Nick were twisted in the duvet, arms around each other, legs woven one on top of the other.

Their lovemaking was over, but she was still floating in euphoria. He'd said she'd looked wild and sexy, but even better, he'd made her feel that way.

She splayed a hand over his chest, feeling the hard muscle under the skin and, beneath that, the thudding of his heart, regular and strong. If only he could be that sort of man, too. She knew he had the potential. But only time would tell if he intended to live up to it.

"You okay?" he asked.

"Oh, yes." She could feel him twisting a strand of her hair with his fingers. She'd never had a lover so enthralled with her hair. He'd gone crazy when she'd spilled it over his body as he came.

She rolled onto her side, curving her body right into his. She was starting to come off her high, but she wasn't worried that she would regret this in the morning.

She wouldn't have missed making love with Nick for the world. She wanted it to happen again. She *longed* for it to happen again. But even if it didn't. Even if this turned out like their first kiss—more of an experiment than anything else—she was glad it had happened.

She finally understood what true passion was like.

"Bridge?"

"Yes?"

"Do you want to spend Christmas together? You could come to my brother's. My family would love to meet you."

Her heart caught at the invitation. "That sounds nice. What about Christmas Eve? I usually go to my parents, but I was thinking of inviting them here for a change."

"Meet the parents. Yeah. That's a good idea, too."

"I should probably warn you. It won't be fun. My father will fuss about my wasted education. And before you know it, Mom will be mooning over Troy again and saying what a shame it is that the two of us never married."

"That sounds grim," he agreed. "But the Gray family is no picnic, either. I'll tell my brothers to go easy on you."

Bridget closed her eyes. Nick was running his fingers lightly over her back and the sensation was hypnotic. She thought she dozed for a while. Maybe an hour. Her next conscious thought was of feeling cold.

She blinked and tried to orient herself in the dark room.

Nick was untangling himself from the duvet.

"I'm going to check on Mandy, then get some water. Want a glass?"

"No," she murmured, her eyes already floating closed again.

A DIM GLOW from the hallway night-light illuminated Bridget's face. The little bump on the bridge of her nose. The scattering of freckles, the fan of her eye-lashes. Nick looked without touching for a few minutes. He'd never experienced this kind of desire before. The kind that laced tenderness with passion, and giving with need. He felt there was something important he had to tell her. At the same time, he worried that words would only spoil the moment.

Tonight had been different, right from the start. Acknowledging this, he found he didn't want to dwell on it. He went to check on his daughter and found her sleeping soundly. Somehow he knew that she wouldn't be waking up until morning. Like him, she slept better at Bridget's.

ON FRIDAY Nick awoke to find Bridget tying the sash of her silk robe. She was in front of the mirror and he could see her face in the reflection, as well as a rear view. Not a bad way to wake up. Certainly beat his usual morning radio program.

"Morning, beautiful."

She picked something off the floor. Next thing he knew a pillow was flying at him. He caught it with ease and set it aside. "Do compliments always set you off like that?"

"Not if they're genuine."

"Huh?"

"You forget. I've seen the women you've dated. Most could be models or movie stars."

"Get real, Bridget." He didn't like the way that made him seem. Like he was shallow or something.

Guilty as charged?

He got out of bed and pulled on his pants. "Is Mandy up yet?"

"I'll go check."

As soon as Bridget was out of the room, Nick thought about Tara Lang. If his theory was correct, today would be the day Colin Porter picked up a rental car and drove Tara God only knows where.

He had to make sure that didn't happen.

But first he needed a shower and some clean clothes.

Bridget returned, with a finger pressed to her lips. "Mandy's still asleep."

"Good," he said, though he found it dispiriting that his daughter seemed to have no problems sleeping through the night anywhere but at his place.

He ran a hand through his hair and felt the strands stick straight up. Bridget, watching, laughed. "I think you need a shower."

"No compliments for me this morning?" He went to her and looped his arms around her waist. "So what's the verdict? Are we okay?"

"What do you mean?"

"You and me. Are we okay?"

"You and me are great," she said softly.

"Good." He gave her a hug. "I'll save my kisses until I've had a chance to brush my teeth." He snagged his watch which he'd left on her bedside table. "I'm going to be staking out Colin Porter's house later this afternoon. I'm not sure when I'll be able to pick up Mandy."

"That's okay, Nick. Stay as long as you need to. You know Mandy will be safe with me."

AFTER THE MORNING BRIEFING, Nick grabbed a couple of coffees and went to talk to his partner. "Did you manage to track down the songbird yesterday?"

"Yeah." Glenn was having one of his good days. He'd shaved and showered and his shirt must have come straight from the cleaners, it was so crisp.

"Well? Any luck?"

"Not as far as Tara Lang is concerned. But the guy makes a hobby out of chatting up young girls on the Internet. I'm planning to keep an eye on him."

"Sounds like a good idea."

"What about you? Still think the Lang girl is holed up with her English teacher?"

"I'm betting on it. I'm headed out to his place now. School doesn't let out for the holidays until three. But I'm worried Porter might decide to slip out early."

He couldn't risk missing his one chance to keep Tara from leaving the state and, therefore, the jurisdiction of the Hartford Police Department.

"Okay," Glenn said. "Let me know if you need any backup. I've got a bunch of calls to make. I should be at my desk most of the day."

An hour later, Nick parked his car several houses down from Porter's apartment building. Lucky for him, one of the home owners on the street was in the midst of a renovation. His car blended in nicely with the service vehicles parked out front.

He'd expected to have to while away several hours and so he'd brought paperwork along, as well as some snacks and a bottle of water. No coffee. Though the caffeine would be appreciated, the lack of washroom facilities in his car made drinking coffee a bad idea.

After a few hours, one of the construction workers came out to the street to get something from his truck. He gave Nick a curious glance. Nick flashed his badge. The guy nodded, then hurried along.

Shortly after noon a figure emerged from the front door of the apartment building. He recognized the dark spiky hair from his sighting at the bookstore and his adrenaline soared.

Tara. He'd been right. Or, rather, Bridget had been right. After all, she'd been the one to point him in Colin's direction.

Nick eased out of his car. The runaway teenager was dressed in her winter jacket and carrying her backpack. She started purposefully down the street, walking away from him.

Had she come to her senses and decided to return home? Or had Porter made plans for her to meet him someplace else?

Nick moved slowly, trying not to attract attention as he moved toward her. But Tara caught sight of him and started to run.

"Tara, wait! It's the police. I just want to help you."

She continued to bolt, darting through a hedge, slipping around a corner. He hurried to make up the hundred yards she had on him, taking the same corner about ten seconds later. He realized Tara had planned her exit from Porter's apartment perfectly. A city bus was just pulling up to the curb.

Tara tossed him a look over her shoulder, then jumped onto the bus. The doors were slamming shut, just as Nick arrived. He made eye contact with the driver, who sighed, then reopened the doors.

There were only a handful of people sitting on the bench seats. Nick started down the aisle until he found her at the very back, head turned to face the side window.

"Tara Lang?"

She froze at the sound of her name but didn't make any other acknowledgment of his presence.

"Don't be afraid. I'm Nick Gray, a detective with the Hartford Police Department. Are you all right?"

After a long moment she nodded.

"I saw you at the bookstore the other night."

She nodded again.

"Your mother is very worried about you, Tara."

She looked fine, he noticed with relief. Healthy. No bruises. At least none that he could see.

"Yeah? What about my dad? I saw him on TV last night. He didn't look too upset."

"Men have different ways of coping with stress."

She didn't buy the explanation. "Give me a break. I know exactly what he's worried about. That I won't be home in time to go to the mayor's Christmas party."

He couldn't argue with her on that. "Well, what about your mother? Trust me, she is falling apart over this."

Tara's bottom lip trembled. "I'll phone her, okay? Just leave me alone. I'm not going back to that house."

"Where *are* you going? Are you on your way to meet Mr. Porter?"

Her eyes widened and he knew right away that his hunch had been correct. "Where is he planning to take you? Has he told you?"

She shrugged her shoulders. "I don't want to talk to you about this."

"Tara, did he hurt you?"

"No! He's so nice. No one has ever been that nice to me before."

"Tara, what exactly is the relationship between you and Mr. Porter?"

"He's my teacher." In a quieter voice she added, "And my friend."

"Friend? Tara, do you know how old Mr. Porter is? He's thirty-two. Almost double your age."

"It doesn't matter. We talk. And watch movies."

Yeah, Nick could just imagine. "Did he tell you to run away from home?"

"I wasn't supposed to go so soon. I was supposed to wait until school break. We were going to go on a holiday together. But I had a fight with my Dad and I couldn't wait. Colin didn't get mad. He let me stay with him. He didn't even get mad when I slipped out to go to the mall when I wasn't supposed to."

"Why does Colin want to go on a holiday with you, Tara? Did he tell you?"

"Don't look at me that way. I know what you're thinking. And it isn't like that. *He* isn't like that."

"Are you sure?"

Tara turned away without answering. But in her

lap, her hands twisted, the knuckles white with tension. And after a moment, he saw a tear drop from her chin.

Nick handed her a tissue, then pulled out his phone and placed a call to Glenn. "I'm with Tara Lang," he said. "I want you to go to the school right now and arrest Colin Porter before he has a chance to get away."

"What are you doing?" Tara pushed at him, trying to get him away from her. "Colin didn't do anything wrong! You can't arrest him!"

Enduring the teenager's shoving and tears, Nick waited for her to calm down. Once she was quiet again, he said softly, "Honey, do you really not understand what his motives were?"

She started crying again. "It wasn't like that." And then, a moment later, she said, "I want to see my mom."

"Don't worry," he said. "My partner's already called her. She'll probably be at the police station before we are."

ANNABEL LANG ARRIVED at police headquarters twenty minutes after Glenn placed his call to her. Clearly she hadn't taken the time to change or put on makeup. She looked disheveled and distraught—much as she had the last time Nick spoke with her.

She held out her arms and Tara didn't hesitate to go to her. As they hugged, she smiled gratefully at Nick.

"Were you able to reach your husband?" he asked.

She shook her head in the negative, the smile disappearing. "I couldn't get through to him."

Earlier, he'd asked Tara if she'd wanted to call her father. She'd said a definite no.

"May I take her home?" Annabel was obviously in a hurry to leave. Partly, Nick was sure, because of her daughter. But also, he suspected, because she felt uncomfortable being out in public in her present state.

"Tara needs to give us her statement," he said. "Tara, would you like your mother to be present?" When she nodded, he led the two of them to the small conference room where an officer was prepared with the necessary paperwork.

"Let me get you some coffee," he offered. "Tara, would you like a cola?"

"Yes, please. Diet if you have it."

Nick made his way to the break room. A general air of relief permeated the department. Chief Wilson was in his office, no doubt trying to reach Vincent Lang to report the good news. His daughter was being returned to him, and right in time for the mayor's Christmas party, too.

Glenn hadn't returned with Colin Porter, yet. He'd taken another detective with him. Nick hoped they hadn't run into any problems.

When he returned with the coffee, Annabel thanked him. Considering the fact that she'd just been reunited with her daughter, she didn't look as pleased as he would have expected.

He sat in the chair next to her and waited until the statement had been signed. When Tara asked to use the washroom, he found two chairs where he and Annabel could sit to wait.

They were silent for a while, then she said, "Thank you for not telling anyone what I did."

"You mean alerting the media? No problem."

"You understand why I had to do it secretly."

"Not really."

She sighed but didn't explain. A moment later she said, "Tara doesn't want to go back home."

"She told me the same thing. We talked a lot on the bus ride downtown. It sounds like there are some real issues with her father. Issues that border on abuse."

He waited for Annabel to deny the problems, but she didn't.

"What should I do, Detective? What would you do if you were me?"

"I'm sorry, Mrs. Lang. But I have to tell you that if things don't change at your house, I think Tara's a high risk to run again. Family counseling might help."

"Not an option."

Nick supposed it wouldn't fit with the family image Vincent Lang was so desperate to portray. "If your daughter is this unhappy, do you have a choice?"

"Vincent won't go for it."

"Counseling is pretty mainstream now. Lots of average men and women can relate to having a troublesome teenager."

"It doesn't matter. Average means nothing to Vincent. He accepts only the best."

Which meant she had to be the best wife. Tara the best child. "Those are impossible standards."

"Yes." As she spoke, Tara emerged from the washroom. Annabel stood and held out her hand to her daughter. After a brief hesitation, Tara took it.

"Mom...? Do we have to go home?"

"Yes. Don't worry, honey. It'll be okay."

Annabel's voice was soothing but her troubled expression did not give Nick a good feeling in his gut.

CHAPTER SEVENTEEN

NICK KNEW that Bridget would be waiting anxiously for word about Tara, but he didn't want to give her the news over the phone. He managed to get away from the station just before six.

Bridget met him at the door. "Well?"

"We found her."

"Really? Oh, Nick, I'm so glad. Come in and tell me all about it."

"I will," Nick promised. But first he needed to hold his daughter close. Bridget seemed to understand how he felt, giving them a moment alone while she puttered in the kitchen.

Nick kissed the top of Mandy's head. He thought about some of the things Tara had told him on their long ride to the police station. Her father had failed her in ways she didn't even understand yet. Maybe Nick could avoid some of those mistakes with Mandy. But he might make others and not even realize what he was doing wrong.

Fatherhood was a bloody terrifying proposition. Why hadn't either of his brothers warned him about this?

"Nick?" Bridget emerged from the kitchen. "Are you okay? I was going to make some pasta for myself—Mandy has already eaten. Would you like some, too?"

He smiled gratefully. "I'm starving. Thanks, that would be great."

Though he couldn't be much help with Mandy in his arms, Nick kept Bridget company in the kitchen while she prepared the meal. He filled her in on the details of the day, including Annabel and Tara's reunion. "Tara was glad to see her mother, but she wasn't happy about going home."

"Vincent Lang is not a good father," Bridget said, punctuating her comment with a wave of her wooden spoon. "He isn't a good husband, either."

"Yeah. Tara told me enough to make me concerned. She says he's never hurt her, not physically, anyway."

Bridget nodded. "Annabel's told me the same thing. The marriage has been in trouble for years. She can't decide whether to stay or to go. She says if Vincent ever hit Tara, she'd leave in an instant. She doesn't seem to understand that verbal abuse is just as harmful."

"Tara's emotional scars made her especially susceptible to a predator like Colin."

"What happened with him, anyway? Has he been arrested?"

"Not yet. My partner and another officer went to the school to apprehend him, but he'd already left. His apartment is being watched, but so far he hasn't appeared. When he does, though, we'll nab him."

"Good."

Nick looked at her thoughtfully. "You know, I never would have figured out what Porter was up to without your help."

She shook her head, as if rejecting her role. "You did all the work, Nick."

"Only because you pointed me in the right direction." He couldn't believe he was the one defending her numerology now, but he couldn't deny that it had worked in this case. "If you hadn't insisted I take a closer look at him, I never would have singled out Colin Porter for investigation. If not for you, Tara might be with him right now, getting into a situation far worse than the one she was leaving behind."

"I can't stand to think about that."

For a second there was silence. And suddenly he wasn't thinking about the case anymore—he was just thinking about her and how amazing she was. Not to mention sexy. He loved that she was cooking in her bare feet, a white apron tied to her waist. "The steam from the pasta is making your hair curl."

She tucked a strand behind her ear.

"Don't do that." He switched Mandy to his other arm, so he could lean over and kiss her. "I like your wild and sexy look."

"I'm beginning to get that message."

"Good. So…where are the dogs? Have they all gone home for the holidays?"

"Every last one of them. Even Lefty's owner managed to pick him up early today."

"Sounds like you're going to have extra time on

your hands. I have some ideas on how to fill it." He tried to give her a sexy grin, but it was difficult with Mandy pulling on his ear.

"So do I."

"Yeah? Let's hear them."

"Well…I don't have a turkey, yet."

"Bridge, those are not the sort of ideas I was looking for. But your kitchen does have some potential. I think we could have fun with that apron, for instance."

"Nick. Not in front of Mandy." She took the baby's little hands in hers. "We are going to have so much fun this Christmas. And we'll take lots of pictures, so when you're older you'll see you had the best first Christmas, ever."

Nick rolled his eyes. He had to keep up his image. But the truth was, he was excited, too.

NOW THAT NICK and Mandy were officially part of her life, there was no way Bridget was going to let Nick's minimalistic approach dilute her enthusiasm for the holidays.

Over the next few days they took Mandy to church so she could hear real Christmas carols. They bundled her up and went sledding on a gentle hill in the neighborhood park. They even lined up for a photo with Santa at the mall. Mandy was a little nervous so Nick held her, while Bridget sat on Santa's knee and told him what *she* wanted for Christmas.

"I think I've already got it," she whispered, her eyes on Nick.

Every night they watched a different Christmas

movie. *Miracle on 34th Street, The Grinch Who Stole Christmas, The Polar Express*. And then, once Mandy was asleep, they made love.

Nick didn't complain about the holidays once. Indeed, he seemed to cherish all the time he spent with his daughter. And he made good use of the times they were alone, too.

The only thing that could have made the holidays better would have been hearing that Colin Porter had been arrested. But as the days passed with no sign of him, Nick became convinced that he'd left the city as he'd planned...only, thankfully, without Tara.

BY QUARTER TO SIX on Christmas Eve, Nick was sorry he'd ever agreed to attend dinner with Bridget's parents. Normally so happy and easygoing, Bridget had been a bear all day. Instead of going on a long walk with Mandy and him, she'd stayed home to dust and vacuum, even though her house was already perfectly clean as far as he could tell.

She was going crazy about the dinner, too. She'd driven halfway across the city to buy prawns from a particular shop, then almost the same distance to choose cheeses to follow the main course.

Her cupboards were full of Christmas baking, but none of it was deemed suitable for dessert tonight. No, that had to come from a snooty bakery, the kind where you had to order a week in advance, unless you groveled and were willing to take whatever they would give you.

In this case, it was lemon tart, which Bridget said

would be perfect with fresh raspberries. Only the local market hadn't carried those, either, so that had entailed another long drive…

Now, as Bridget fussed with the table settings, Nick was trying to keep Mandy and himself out of her way. He fed Mandy early, then dressed her in the cute outfit Bridget had set out on the spare bed.

His clothes, too, had been chosen by Bridget. Earlier, he'd asked her if she'd written him a script for the evening. She hadn't been amused.

As he stepped into the pants Bridget had carefully pressed, Nick realized that despite all her disparaging comments, her parents' opinions were important to her.

Which meant that what they thought of *him* was important, too.

Suddenly Nick felt a little queasy. He'd always had good luck with women. But with parents…not so much. He tucked in his shirt, tightened his belt. "What do you think, Mandy?" he asked his daughter, who was sitting on a blanket on the floor. "Does your old man look respectable?"

Seeing that he was smiling, she smiled, too.

God, if it could always be this easy.

He was just reaching for his phone, intending to clip it to his belt, when it rang. Hoping to hear that Porter had been apprehended, Nick flipped it open.

"Gray here."

"It's me. Jessica. Merry Christmas, Nick."

He did a quick calculation and realized it would be Christmas afternoon where she was. "Same to you. Mandy's fine. She's smiling at me right now."

"Where are you guys? I called your home number first. I was surprised when no one answered. Are you at one of your brothers'?"

"Actually, I'm at my girlfriend's. Bridget Humphrey."

"Isn't that the name of the sitter you hired to look after Mandy?"

"Yeah."

"And now you're sleeping with her. God, you don't change, do you, Nick?"

"It's not like that—"

"Come on, Nick. With you it's always *like that*."

"Not this time."

"Right. Well, give Mandy a hug for me. Tell her that her mama misses her, but that I'll be home soon."

He said a curt farewell, then pocketed his phone. Damn it. He'd been in a good mood until he'd talked to her. Where did she get off judging his relationship with Bridget? He'd bet that as soon as this trip was over, she'd forget all about her snowboarding lover Will—or was it Bill?

By the time the doorbell rang, he was almost as jittery as Bridget was. He set Mandy on her favorite spot on the white rug, and waited while Bridget let her parents in. He heard the murmur of voices, and then footsteps. He smiled as the tall, older couple entered the room.

Before Bridget had a chance to introduce them, her mother noticed Mandy cooing happily on the floor. Her eyes widened. "Bridget? What's this?"

"A baby, Mom. She's Nick's daughter, Mandy. And this is the guy I was telling you about. Nick Gray, I'd like you to meet my mother, Clarissa, and my father, Graham."

Nick generally enjoyed meeting new people. Not the Humphreys. They turned a cold eye to his smile, and it seemed nothing he said elicited much more than a grunt from her father.

He helped Bridget serve drinks, then waited until everyone was seated before he took an armchair for himself.

Her parents both wore glasses and were slender. He couldn't see any similarity between them and their daughter. Though he suspected that when Graham Humphrey was younger, his hair might have been red, also.

The Humphreys had settled into either end of the sofa as if their spines had calcified. Noticing how they were dressed—Bridget's father in gray slacks and a blazer, her mother in a dark green velvet dress—Nick was thankful Bridget had chosen his clothing for him.

He took a deep breath and told himself to relax. This was supposed to be fun. But he'd felt more at ease interrogating criminals.

"So, Nick." Graham lifted his chin, achieving the effect of looking down at him, even though Nick was the taller of the two. "What business are you in?"

"I'm a cop."

"Oh," the Humphreys said, simultaneously.

"He was just promoted to detective. You must

have heard about the Tara Lang case in the news. Nick is the one who found her."

"How impressive," Clarissa said, her tone belying her words.

"Your daughter helped, actually," Nick said. He was about to explain about how she'd used numerology to zero in on the right suspect, when he noticed Bridget drawing her finger across her throat.

He aborted the story, and finished with a lame explanation about how she'd had a hunch that had really paid off. The Humphreys looked bored.

The conversation did not improve from there. Once he'd put Mandy to bed for the night, they sat down to the dinner Bridget had fussed over. Bridget asked for his help carrying out the salad plates. In the kitchen she whispered, "I'm so sorry."

He kissed her gently. "Don't worry. I'm a big boy. And they're only acting this way because they want the best for you."

Despite his reassuring words, though, the Humphreys' coldness—and occasional rudeness— grated. Clarissa found something to criticize with every course. He felt badly for Bridget's sake. She had tried so hard to make the evening perfect. But so far, her parents hadn't made one positive comment.

The conversation centered around an opera he hadn't seen, books he hadn't read and people he'd never met. When Bridget admitted she hadn't read the latest literary sensation, her mother shook her head. "Still wasting your time with those historical romances?"

Nick leaned over to give her a kiss. "She's making time for some modern romance, too."

No one seemed to find his comment even moderately amusing.

Finally the dinner drew to a close. Bridget brought out the cheese plate and asked Nick to pour the port. He had never had port before and found it too sweet for his taste. But the Humphreys seemed to like it. Finally, something they approved of.

After her second glass, Clarissa leaned toward her daughter. "Did you hear that Troy Whitman is switching companies? He's going to be a vice president now." She turned to Nick, explaining, "Troy is an old boyfriend of Bridget's." She held her fingers a hairbreadth apart. "They came this close to getting married."

Nick mustered a smile, hoping to demonstrate to Bridget that her parents' behavior wasn't bothering him in the least.

In fact, he wasn't sure how much more he could take. Bridget's parents were snobs, no doubt about it. And it was just as clear that they didn't like him. But maybe they were justified. Bridget obviously came from an intellectual, privileged background. She was a Harvard grad, a lovely person, the kind of woman any guy would be lucky to marry.

What did he have to offer her? Not money, that was for sure. He had a failed marriage behind him, a baby daughter, and no track record of reliability where women were concerned.

On top of that, there was his job. Being a cop was

demanding, exciting and challenging from his perspective. But he'd heard his colleagues' spouses complain about the irregular hours, the daily possibility of danger, the psychological toll from dealing with the reality of the street. All these placed an enormous strain on a cop's personal relationships.

No wonder her parents weren't giving him their stamp of approval.

When Graham Humphrey began talking about the career success of Bridget's other long-term boyfriend, Nick was relieved to feel his cell phone vibrating in his pocket. Normally he would have ignored it until everyone had left the table. But tonight he pulled it out.

"Please excuse me. This could be important."

Bridget's eyes begged him not to go as he left the table. He winked, as if to tell her not to worry, then went to her office and closed the door.

CHAPTER EIGHTEEN

WHY HAD SHE TAKEN so many pains with this meal? She should have known it would go this way. Next year she'd save herself the bother and just show up at her mother and father's for Christmas Eve dinner.

As the minutes dragged on, Bridget wondered what was keeping Nick on the phone. Could he possibly have rigged the thing to go off just so he could escape from the table?

If he had, she wouldn't blame him. Her parents were in especially fine form tonight.

Her father had just started on his lecture about her choice of career, when Nick finally reappeared. He'd removed his tie, loosened his shirt and was clipping his phone back onto his belt. She could tell by the light in his eyes that he was slipping into detective mode.

"That was work. We've got a possible sighting on Porter. I need to go check it out right away."

"Oh, Nick." She wanted Porter found and taken into custody. But did it have to be now? And by him?

"I'm sorry, Bridge. Sorry, Mr. and Mrs. Humphrey."

"You're leaving now?" Clarissa Humphrey was astonished. "On Christmas Eve?"

"Afraid so. It was nice to meet you both. Bridget—" he leaned in toward her "—what would you like me to do about Mandy? I could call my brother—"

"Don't be silly, Nick. Leave her here. How long do you think you'll be?"

"Impossible to say. I'll call you as soon as I know." He kissed her lightly and squeezed her shoulder. And then he was gone.

As soon as the door had closed behind him, her mother raised her eyebrows. "This is what it'll be like being married to a cop, Bridget. At least you know what you're getting into."

NICK HAD NEVER BEEN so glad to get an after-hours call in his life. As he drove toward the address of the bar Glenn had given him, he felt the tension from the long, dull evening slide away. Christmas lights flashed around him as he maneuvered through the streets of his city. Soon he was parked in front of the Rusty Nail. To him, it didn't seem like the sort of establishment that Colin Porter would frequent.

But then, Colin Porter wouldn't be hanging out at his regular establishments if he was smart. And there was little doubt that he was that.

Nick slipped in the main door, senses on high alert. He scanned the patrons but saw no sign of the slight English teacher.

He had no trouble spotting Glenn, though. His partner was at the bar with two empty glasses lined up in front of him.

Nick slid into an empty seat. "So. What's happening?"

"Not much. The call came in about half an hour ago, so we might have missed him. But I'm thinking it might have been a mistaken ID. See that guy in the corner?"

Nick slowly rotated his head in the right direction. The man was slight of build, with Porter's coloring and nondescript features. Someone who'd only seen Porter's photograph could easily mistake him for their guy.

"I didn't figure this would be Porter's kind of joint anyway."

Glenn nodded. "Crowd's too old."

Nick's shoulders slumped at the reminder of Porter's preference…jailbait. It was enough to make him sick.

"Since you're here…how about a drink? On me, because it's Christmas."

Before Nick could object, Glenn had ordered him a Bud. Nick sank into his seat. Maybe he'd stay for one. It couldn't hurt. Besides, he felt badly for Glenn. All alone on Christmas Eve.

He glanced around. The place was surprisingly full. Didn't these people have someplace better to go?

Don't you?

He swallowed his guilt with his first swig of beer. The anxiety and stress that had been building all day were finally out of his system and he could see the situation more clearly now that he had some distance.

He didn't blame Bridget's folks for being jerks. They wanted what was best for their daughter, and clearly they didn't think a cop with the baggage of a failed marriage and a six-month-old baby qualified.

He could live with their disapproval if he knew they were wrong. But damn it, Bridget was smart as well as good-hearted and beautiful. Why was she wasting her time with him?

"Want another?" Glenn asked.

"Yeah. I think I do."

BRIDGET COULDN'T WAIT for her parents to leave and, fortunately, they obliged her by making their excuses about a half hour after Nick's departure. She handed them their gifts at the door and accepted from her father the card that would contain the customary check they gave her each Christmas.

As soon as they were gone, she changed from her dress into her most comfortable flannel pajamas. What a dreadful evening. A disaster on all fronts. Maybe she should have done a better job of warning Nick about her parents, but she'd tried.

She couldn't help believing that he'd used that call as an excuse to get out of here. Couldn't he have stuck it out just one more hour? But Nick Gray wasn't the kind of guy who stuck out the hard times in a relationship. He was probably already trying to decide who the next woman in his life would be.

Or was she being uncharitable? Maybe he was arresting Colin Porter right this very second. She should wait before she assumed the worst.

Once she'd cleaned the kitchen, Bridget went to the spare room where Mandy was sleeping. She looked so content, one chubby little hand tucked under her chin. Such an adorable baby. Did Nick realize how lucky he was?

Bridget noticed a tear drop to the flannel blanket. She put a finger to her eye and felt dampness. Was she crying for Mandy? Or for herself?

She left the little girl in peace, went around her home turning out lights until all that was left were the multicolored strands on the Christmas tree. When would Nick be coming home? He hadn't said and still hadn't called. She picked up the portable telephone, then settled with a blanket on the sofa.

The Christmas lights were so pretty, promising the comfort and joy that everyone associated with the season. But she had offered all that to Nick. And still he'd gone running.

Please phone me. She closed her eyes. Willed him to hear her, wherever he was. *Let me be wrong. Let him be working.* And finally… *Let him be safe.*

Bridget slept.

An hour later the phone rang. She was instantly awake. "Hello?"

"Bridge? It's Nick."

He'd been drinking. A lot. She could hear it in his fuzzy enunciation and the fake cheerfulness of his voice.

"Where are you?"

"Not sure. Hang on." She heard a blend of music and voices in the background, then Nick's voice. "Which bar are we at now, Glenn?"

There was mumbling, then Nick was back on the line. "I'm at Coach's Sports Bar, downtown. Not that far away."

Some of the voices she'd heard were female. Was one of them sitting beside him right now? Damn him for doing this to her. For making her feel so alone and...jealous.

"What about Colin Porter?"

"It was a mistake. Some guy who looked like him. Glenn was here and I didn't want him to be alone so I stayed for a few drinks."

A few. Right.

"I haven't forgotten Mandy. I'm going to call a cab and come and get her right now."

"Don't. Let her sleep. You can pick her up in the morning." He'd thought of Mandy. But not her.

"Okay. Thanks, Bridge."

She had no answer to that so she hung up.

A BABY'S CRY WAS the first thing Bridget heard on Christmas morning. She woke with a sore neck. The sofa was definitely not that comfortable. She rose quickly and hurried to the spare room.

"Hi, sweetie. Merry Christmas."

Bridget plucked Mandy from the crib and even the baby's instant smile was not enough to ease the pain gripping Bridget's heart right now.

This was not the Christmas morning she had

dreamed about. For days she'd been looking forward to waking in Nick's arms, to a stolen kiss before they rescued Mandy from her crib and went to see what Santa had brought.

Nothing, Bridget realized sadly. The stocking Nick had purchased for his daughter was still lying limp by the Christmas tree. He'd told her he would buy some cute little toys, but he must have forgotten.

He hadn't said anything about the puppy, either. He must have decided it was too big a commitment.

Of course she had some wrapped gifts for the baby under the tree. But that wasn't the same.

Bridget prepared the special Christmas breakfast she'd been planning. Who cared if Nick wasn't here for his daughter's first ever Christmas morning? The way he'd sounded last night, he'd be lucky to make it for noon.

Where had he spent the night? Could he possibly have picked up one of the women at the bar last night? The possibility that Nick might be, right this minute, in bed with another woman made her so furious and sad she felt like being sick.

In the end, she ate nothing and fed Mandy the same boring cereal and formula the baby had every day for breakfast. She looked ruefully at the untouched spread on the table, then brought a spoonful of the pabulum to Mandy's lips. "Some Christmas, huh, Mandy?"

For Mandy's sake, Bridget put carols on the sound system. Mandy reacted instantly to the joyous music and Bridget was glad she'd made the effort.

Every few minutes or so, Bridget would think of Nick, and a raw pain like sandpaper on a wound had her catching her breath.

How could he? How could he? How could he?

She'd been deluding herself about Nick. Maybe he liked dogs and babies, but he was not the man she'd hoped he would be. Not even deep, deep inside. His specialty was short-term relationships. Period. She'd known that from the beginning. She had only herself to blame for expecting more.

Bridget pushed aside her hurt feelings and tried to focus on Mandy. She photographed the baby by the tree, surrounded by the wrapped presents Bridget had bought her. Then Bridget unwrapped each gift, giving Mandy the paper and ribbons to play with.

They were just opening the last present when the doorbell rang.

CHAPTER NINTEEN

BRIDGET WAS EXPECTING to see a contrite Nick on her doorstep, but it was Annabel Lang. Though she was bundled into a thick fur coat, she shivered in the cold.

"Annabel. What's wrong?"

"It's Tara. She's run away again."

"Oh, no. Come in." Once she'd removed her coat and boots, Bridget invited her to sit on the sofa. Mandy smiled at the new person in the room, then went back to playing with the ribbon and wrapping paper.

"This is Mandy. She's a friend's daughter." Bridget settled next to Annabel on the sofa and placed a comforting hand on her shoulder. "What happened?"

"Oh, Bridget. I was so happy to have Tara home again. And I thought Vincent was, too. He was kind and concerned...and he even hugged her."

How sad that a hug from her father should be worthy of mention, Bridget thought.

"I hoped that maybe this would be a turning point for him—for the entire family. But then, on Sunday morning Tara informed us that she would not be attending the mayor's Christmas party. Vincent went ballistic. I'm sure he would have hurt

Tara if we hadn't had staff in the house. He threatened her with everything...loss of her cell phone, no more allowance, no summer vacation at the horse ranch she loves so much. But Tara wouldn't change her mind."

"That must have taken guts."

Annabel nodded. "I hate to admit this, but I tried to talk her into compromising. Go to this function, I told her, and it will be the only holiday party you have to attend."

"She wouldn't listen to you, either?"

"Actually, she did. She went to the mayor's party, and she was miserable, and it was obvious to everyone who saw her. Vincent acted the part of the indulgent, understanding parent. He told everyone that she'd been through a lot and wasn't quite herself yet."

"True enough," Bridget said.

"But when we got home..." Annabel shuddered as her voice trailed off.

Bridget dreaded hearing the rest. "Did he hurt her?"

"Yes," Annabel whispered. "Tara didn't come out of her room for three days. I couldn't even coax her out for Christmas Eve dinner. And then, when I checked this morning...she was gone. Oh, Bridget, what am I going to do? I may have really lost her this time."

Annabel started weeping then, and Bridget held her close, trying to offer comfort.

"I'm so sorry, Annabel." She would have loved to say something to make her feel better. But what could she say? Especially when she knew Colin Porter was still on the loose.

NICK'S CELL PHONE was ringing. He'd been sleeping soundly—or was it passed out?—in his own bed. The jarring sound triggered his reflexes and he jerked upright, swearing as pain ricocheted through his brain.

He grabbed hold of the phone just in time. "Nick Gray here."

"Detective Gray?"

He'd been expecting Bridget. He'd been intending to grovel. Now he mentally switched gears, quickly placing the voice. "Is this Tara Lang?"

"I'm in trouble."

"What happened?"

"I ran away again. I called Colin."

Damn it. "Tara, where are you? I'll come and get you right away." He couldn't believe she'd ended up in the exact same predicament. What a bloody mess. If she had a decent father...

The shame of how he'd spent the past ten hours hit Nick then. He lowered his head, wincing at the memory of the bars, the drinks, the woman with brown eyes and long legs who'd tried to convince him to go home with her.

Thank God, he'd drawn the line there, at least.

"Tara, after you called Colin, where did you go?"

"He told me to meet him at the Golden Night Motel. So I did. I took a cab."

Oh, God. From the frying pan to the fire. "This was last night?"

"Yeah."

He didn't want to think about what might have happened. "Are you still in the room?"

"No. We're at a coffee shop near the highway. Colin still wants us to go on that holiday we talked about. He's picked up a rental car and right now he's buying sandwiches and snacks for the drive."

"Where is he planning to take you?"

"I don't know. It was supposed to be a surprise, which seemed exciting before, but now, I'm not so sure. Last night was weird. Colin was trying super hard to be nice, but I think he's actually kind of angry at me. I kept remembering what you'd said to me. That there was a reason an older man would be interested in a girl like me, and—" She stopped, hiccupping over a sob.

"Where, exactly, are you right now?"

"In the restroom at the coffee shop. This nice woman let me use her phone."

"Do you know the address of the coffee shop?"

"It's just off Interstate 84. The Golden Night Motel and a McDonald's are across the street."

"I know the place." Nick was already out of bed, scrambling into his jeans, while propping the phone between his ear and his shoulder. "Stay in the ladies' room, Tara. Lock yourself into a stall and don't come out for anyone but me. If someone tries to give you a hard time, give them my number and tell them to call me. I'll be there as soon as I can."

NICK TOOK A TAXI to the bar to retrieve his car, then he called Glenn, hoping his partner was in good enough shape to answer his phone. Glenn sounded impressively sober on the line. When he heard Porter was making a second attempt to kidnap Tara, he was quick to react.

"I'm right behind you, buddy."

As soon as he disconnected from that call, Nick's cell rang again. He glanced down at the display to see Bridget's name and number.

He hated to leave the call to go to messages, but what he had to say to her was too complicated for a time like this. Besides, he needed to think, to plan ahead to what he was going to do once he arrived at the coffee shop.

Porter was smart and he was prepared. The man had a false ID. Would he be armed? Nick would assume yes, until proven otherwise.

Minutes later, he arrived at the Caffeine Zone Coffee Shop. Of the three vehicles in the parking lot, only one was a rental. He parked behind it, blocking it in. As he was getting out from behind the wheel, Glenn drove up. His partner's car screeched to a halt, then Glenn scrambled out to join him.

"Got here as fast as I could. Seen Porter?"

"Not yet. But I figure this is his car." He checked out the coffee shop. There were entrances on both sides of the building. He headed for one and gestured for Glenn to take the other.

His hand was just reaching out toward the door, when it swung open and a man tried to sprint past him. Nick had no time to think. He grabbed the guy's shoulders.

It was Porter. He twisted, struggled, swore. But Nick was taller and much stronger. With little effort, he pinned the man's arms to his side, then swung the slight man around, until his back was locked helplessly against Nick's chest.

"Got him!" he called to Glenn. His partner was already running to his side with the cuffs. As he slipped Porter's wrists into the restraints he began the usual recitation of rights that punctuated every arrest.

Nick tuned him out. "I've got to find Tara."

He rushed into the shop. The clerk behind the counter and two customers were staring. They'd obviously been following the action outside.

"What's going on?" the clerk asked.

Nick ignored the question. "Have you seen a young girl?"

"There's a kid in the washroom." The clerk jerked a thumb to his left.

Nick found Tara locked in a stall as he'd instructed her. He had to coax her out. "It's okay, Tara. Porter's been arrested. He can't hurt you now."

She crept out the door. "I don't want to see him."

"I understand." He shielded her from the window with his body. "Are you all right?"

"Yeah, I guess."

"Good." So often he had to deal with crimes after they were committed. It felt good to have prevented one for a change. He glanced out the window and saw that Glenn had hauled Colin into the back seat of his car. He was on the phone, probably calling for backup.

"Tara, why'd you run again?"

She didn't say anything for a while, then pulled the neck of her sweater over her shoulder to reveal a big ugly bruise.

Hell. A weary disgust washed over him. "Your dad?"

She nodded.

"That looks painful." The real damage, though, would be emotional. What kind of father did this to his kid? His estimation of Vincent Lang, already low, sank further. "Has your father been violent before?"

"Not with me. But I think he hits my mom. I've noticed her wearing a turtleneck on mornings after they've been arguing."

From what he'd seen of Annabel, he'd have to say she fit the profile of an abused wife. Her fear of her husband was very real.

"I don't want to see him ever again. I don't have to, right?"

"It's complicated, but I'll do my best to help you. We have to start by filing a complaint."

"You mean go to the police station? No way."

"It's the best solution, Tara."

"For some people maybe. Not when your dad is the attorney general. You don't think he'll have a story all worked out? No one's going to believe me when I tell them he did this."

God, she was jaded for one so young. "Did your mother see what happened?"

"What if she did? She'll side with him. She always does."

"Not always."

"Oh? Like when?"

Nick weighed his options. He'd promised to keep Annabel's secret. But in this case, he thought she'd want him to tell. "When you went missing, your dad was anxious to keep the story out of the press even though we thought it would be helpful to go public."

"Yeah. He hates it when our family doesn't look perfect."

"Right." She had his motives nailed, unfortunately. "Well, your mother didn't feel the same way. She's the one who leaked the story to the *Courant*. I found a business card from one of the columnists in her office."

"Mom did that?"

"The point is, Tara, she went against your father's wishes to do the best thing for you. Don't you think she deserves another chance to help you?"

"How? What can Mom do to stop him?" Tara seemed tired but resolved when she added, "I'm never going back to that house again. You can't make me."

"I won't," he promised.

"I don't want to go to the police station, either."

He could understand how she felt. "Eventually you'll have to make a statement."

"Does it have to be right now?"

He considered the options. "No. Let's make a pit stop first. After all…it *is* Christmas."

BRIDGET COULDN'T BELIEVE Nick wasn't answering his phone. Was he still too drunk? Or just too embarrassed to face her? If it was only her he was ignoring, she wouldn't mind so much. But what about Mandy? He'd walked out on his own daughter on Christmas Eve and he didn't seem to even care.

Rather than leave another message, Bridget hung up and went back to the living room to check on Annabel and Mandy. They were on the floor playing with Mandy's new Christmas gifts. The stricken mother seemed to be finding solace from interacting with the baby.

"It's almost lunchtime. I'm heating cereal for Mandy. Would you like something, Annabel? I have lots of food."

Annabel was about to turn down her offer, when the doorbell rang. Bridget forced herself to walk, not run, to the door.

Nick was leaning against the door frame, his expression grim. He hadn't shaved, hadn't brushed his short, thick hair. A nervous flutter started in Bridget's stomach. Anger battled with hope. Could he possibly have a good excuse for what he'd done?

And then she saw the girl beside him. Tara looked tired and scared, her skin painfully white in contrast to the dyed darkness of her hair.

"I hope it's okay that I brought her here." Nick's voice sounded rough. And his eyes held so much pain it hurt to look at them. "We didn't know where else to go."

"You came to the right place. Tara…your mother is here."

"She is?" Tara's eyes widened and she started to shake. Bridget stepped out to the stoop and put an arm around the girl. She was wearing a jacket, but the sneakers on her feet were damp from the snow. Bridget pulled her inside, just as Annabel appeared in the foyer.

"Did I hear—" Annabel froze the second she saw Tara.

Her daughter stood motionless, too. Then, finally, she dropped her gaze to the floor. "I'm sorry, Mom."

"Oh, baby." Annabel ran to her daughter and threw her arms around her. "You don't have any reason to be sorry. I should have protected you from him. I'm the one who's sorry. So very, very sorry."

"I hate him. I won't go back."

"I know, sweetheart. Neither will I."

Tara sucked in a breath. "Do you mean that?"

"Yes. I have some money in an account. I've been thinking about this for a while. We'll stay in a hotel until we find a nice place to live. It won't be a big house like before."

"That's okay," Tara said quickly. "Oh, Mom. I'm just so glad." And then she started to cry and didn't stop for a very long time.

CHAPTER TWENTY

BRIDGET WAS avoiding him. She wouldn't meet his gaze and spoke carefully around him. Annabel and Tara were too preoccupied with their predicament to notice the chill, but Nick was very aware.

Now that the adrenaline rush of rescuing Tara was over, his head was pounding again. He tolerated the pain, feeling it was a deserved reminder of how badly he'd screwed up.

While Annabel and her daughter made plans for moving into a hotel, Nick fed his daughter her lunch, then changed her diaper. His daughter held no grudge against him for not being with her on Christmas morning. She grinned at him happily, then fell asleep in his arms when she grew tired.

With her warm, precious body tucked into his chest, he thought of all the ways a father could wound a daughter. He could never imagine physically harming a child the way Vincent Lang had done. Neither could he see himself wanting his kid to act out a role just to support his goals in life.

But there were other hurts a parent could inflict. Unintentional hurts like not being present at the moments that mattered.

The day would come when he would miss an important day like Christmas and Mandy *would* notice and *would* care.

"Okay. We've got a suite booked for the next week," Annabel said, putting down the phone. "We can check in now." She put an arm around her daughter. "I think we could both use a hot shower, then a nap and maybe a movie. Something with a happy ending."

Nick made plans to meet them at the police station the next day. He would need a statement from Tara and he also wanted to suggest Annabel consider a restraining order against her husband.

"Thanks for everything, Bridget." Annabel hugged her, then turned to Nick. "Thank you so much for bringing my daughter home. You are a true hero."

He felt hypocritical accepting the praise. Some hero. He was sure Bridget didn't see him that way.

Bridget had packed a box full of Christmas baking and she pressed it into Tara's hands as they were leaving. "Call me soon, Annabel. Let me know how you're doing."

"I will," she promised. And then they were gone.

BRIDGET WAITED for Nick to say something. He looked absolutely wretched. And she was glad. He darn well deserved to feel wretched.

"Bridge," he finally managed. "I'm sorry about last night. The drinking. Not being here for Mandy in the morning. I'm sorry about it all. If it makes any difference, I've been miserable since the moment I walked out your front door."

"That phone call you took during dinner with my parents. It wasn't work at all, was it?"

"It was. I told the truth about that part. We did have a reported sighting of Porter. But it turned out to be someone who looked like him. I could have been home an hour after I'd left," he admitted.

"But you didn't come back."

"No. My partner and I had a few beers. Then we moved on to another bar. And…the night just slipped away. It was after midnight when I finally called a cab to take me home."

"Is that when you phoned me?"

"Yeah."

"I see." She waited, expecting more, but he just looked at her. She supposed this was where he expected her to lose her temper and tear a strip off him. But she didn't feel angry anymore. Just sad and disappointed.

"Why do you think you did that? Why would you rather spend Christmas Eve at a bar with your partner than at home with your daughter—" she hesitated, gathering her courage "—and me?"

"It wasn't about that. It was about you. And what you deserve. That's what I finally realized last night."

"Because of my parents? They're just snobs, Nick. I'm sorry I invited them over."

"They *are* snobs," he agreed. "But they're also your family. They know you. And they want the best for you. And so do I," he added softly.

"And you're not the best for me?"

"Look at my track record, Bridge. Some men just aren't cut out to be fathers and husbands."

"Well, it's rather late for that discovery. You *are* a father. And no matter what was going on between you and me last night, you should have been there for Mandy this morning."

"You're right. I'm a jerk."

"Don't say that as if it's some sort of excuse. You and I have a choice about whether we're together. Mandy doesn't have a choice. You're her father. That won't change."

"I know. Damn it, I know." He wanted to do better. He *had* to do better. "Last night was a huge screwup. I won't let it happen again."

"I hope not. You have a conflict between independent seven and relational six. Finding the right balance is possible, though."

She saw the confusion on his face.

"I know you don't have much faith in numerology, but it all boils down to this. You have a choice in your life. If you want to be a good father, you can be."

She turned her back to him so he wouldn't see her tears. "You and Mandy should get going. You don't want to be late for Christmas dinner with your family."

"But what are you going to do?"

"Don't worry about me."

"I don't want you to be alone."

"You weren't worried about that last night."

"Bridget, I'm so sorry. I think in the long run you'll be happier this way. I really do."

The man was an idiot. An absolute idiot. He had

no idea how much she loved him, how good he was for her. But if he couldn't see it, then nothing in this world would make their relationship work.

"PASS THE GRAVY, please, Uncle Nick," Derrick asked from his place at the table next to his father.

Nick finished drowning his turkey and mashed potatoes, then handed over the silver pitcher.

"I thought you were bringing your new girlfriend," Derrick added. His eyes were on his plate so he didn't see the glances that were passed around the table by the adults.

Nick gritted his teeth. "She decided to spend the holiday with her family."

It wasn't true, but it was the story he was running with for now. Gavin raised his eyebrows and Matthew shook his head. His brothers were on to him. And so was his mother. She was frowning worriedly at him instead of eating her food. He needed to change the subject.

"Want some peas, Mandy?" He offered some of the mashed vegetables to his daughter, seated in a high chair beside him.

Also at the table was Matt's wife, Jane, Derrick's sister, Violet, Gavin's wife, Allison and their two kids, Tory and baby Jack, also in a high chair like Mandy's.

Lots of family to be grateful for, Nick knew, but right now seeing his brothers with their wives and children only made him feel more inadequate. Why couldn't he be like Matt and Gavin? And their father before them? Was he some sort of genetic mutation?

"You're not eating much, Nick," Jane said quietly, below the murmur of general conversation. "Do you feel okay?"

Actually, his stomach was still upset from the drinking last night. He wasn't used to putting back that much alcohol and today he'd been paying the price. But he couldn't tell Jane he'd gotten hammered on Christmas Eve.

Or maybe he should. Maybe it was time he was completely honest about what a jerk he was.

"Sorry I'm not doing justice to the meal, Jane. I'm a little hungover today."

Everyone turned to look at him. No one had heard Jane's question, but it was just his luck that he'd answered during a lull in the conversation.

"What's hungover, Uncle Nick?" Violet asked, while Derrick smirked.

"It's a type of sickness that happens to people with very bad judgment, honey," Matt said to his daughter, while glaring at his youngest brother. "Where was Mandy while you were…indulging? Let me guess." He snapped his fingers. "You left her with Bridget. No wonder she wouldn't come to dinner with you."

Nick hung his head while his brother pieced together the story for everyone's benefit. He wasn't surprised how quickly Matt figured it out. His brother, unlike him, was a very smart fellow.

"Maybe there's more to the story," Jane said, her eyes lighting on her husband with gentle reprove.

"Yeah, there's more. Nick's sabotaging a great relationship so he can go on being the baby of the family. Why grow up just because you have a daughter to worry about?"

"Stop fighting, boys," said their mother, who looked confused by the conversation but clear about her right to demand civility at the table.

"Mom's right," Gavin said. "Cool it, Matt."

But Nick had already risen from his chair. "Looks like we're low on turkey. I'll carve some more."

He took the platter into the kitchen, then stood in front of the decimated turkey carcass and wondered what was the matter with him. He glanced out the kitchen window. It was snowing again—fat, sloppy flakes, the kind that could make an ordinary city street look magical.

If she were here, Bridget would be pleased.

Nick was just reaching for the knife when Gavin entered the room.

"I have a feeling you shouldn't be near anything sharp right now." He took the knife out of his hands. "You look like you're beating yourself up. Why don't you give yourself a break?"

He started carving more breast meat and Nick used a fork to transfer the slices to the platter. "Matt's right. I had something good this time and I screwed it up."

"I take it Bridget is the something good we're talking about?"

Nick nodded. "She's something else, Gavin. Dogs love her and so do babies. She believes in astrology and numerology, but she also has a physics degree from Harvard. Her parents are the world's worst snobs, but she's the most down-to-earth person you could know."

"I can see why you love her," Gavin said.

"Yeah. But can you see any reason why she would love me?"

"You need to ask *her* that." Gavin set down the knife and clasped Nick's shoulder. "You know that surprise you had set up for later?"

Nick nodded. He'd been so excited a few days ago when he'd had the idea. Not any longer. Mandy would be happy, he knew. But without Bridget the effect wouldn't be the same.

"I think it's time. I'll get Mandy and meet you in the family room."

"Yeah. I suppose." He washed his hands, then took a deep breath. If he was serious about being the best father he could be, then it started here. This was Mandy's first Christmas. Bridget had wanted him to make it special and that was exactly what he intended to do.

Resolutely pushing his bleak mood aside, he forced a smile and made his way to the family room on the other side of the house. He found Mandy there, waiting for him, but she wasn't with Gavin.

Bridget was holding his daughter in her arms.

Looking at her, then, he realized how much he loved her. The potent emotion was like nothing he'd experienced before. It was different than what he felt for Mandy, but just as powerful.

NICK LOOKED TERRIBLE. He still hadn't shaved and his hair was a mess. His face bore the tired lines of a man who had been through an emotional whirlwind. And yet he was smiling, looking at her as if he couldn't believe his eyes.

"What's this? When did you get here?"

"Five minutes ago. Your brother Matt phoned and was very insistent that I come. He even sent a cab." She hesitated, then added, "He said it was a surprise. And would I please give his dumb-ass brother a second chance?"

"Thank God for interfering older brothers. I'm so glad to see you." He stepped toward her, touched her shoulder, then hesitated.

"We need to talk. But first I have to show you something." He went to the corner of the room and pulled out a large, plastic crate. The two puppies must have been sleeping, but as soon as he opened the door they tumbled out to a blanket that had been spread over the carpet.

Gently Nick took Mandy from Bridget's arms. He sat on the carpet by the puppies and settled his daughter on his lap. He scooped up one of the puppies, the one with the white nose and the floppy ears. The puppy licked Mandy's toe and she waved her chubby little arms with excitement.

"Merry Christmas, honey," he said, nuzzling his daughter's soft ear.

Bridget sank down beside them and cupped the second puppy in her hands. "Oh, you're so adorable." She touched her nose to the puppy's soft fawn-colored coat and was rewarded with a wet kiss. Bridget laughed. "You decided to buy Mandy two of these little guys?"

"Actually, that one I bought for you," he said quietly. "If you want her."

Her heart melted then, the last remnant of her anger finally gone. Holding the puppy close, Bridget closed her eyes and nodded. "I do."

"I want a second chance at that apology I gave you earlier."

Bridget opened her eyes, blinking away tears.

"I apologize for running out on you last night. It was a mistake and I'm sorry it happened."

"I understand that my parents were a pain, Nick. But I can't be with someone who runs away from a difficult situation and goes drinking with his buddies."

"I know that, Bridge. And I don't want to be the guy who does that. Trust me, when I'm fifty I don't plan to be living the life that my partner Glenn does."

"I'm glad. But there's something else that has to be said about last night and about this morning. You were so amazing, the way you saved Tara and kept her safe. Nick, maybe you were a jerk last night, but this morning you were a hero. And I'm so proud of you."

"I was just doing my job."

"You were being the man you were meant to be. A man of honor and integrity...just like those brothers you look up to so much."

"I love you, Bridge. I didn't know how much until I thought I'd lost you. I panicked at that dinner with your parents," he added. "I won't do that again. What I need to know, is whether you love me, too?"

As he waited for her answer, she realized he was holding his breath. He really did love her. The thought hit her heart like light on a prism, reflecting happiness through every cell in her body.

"I figure I'm going to be on probation for a while," Nick continued. "But you can count on me. You and Mandy both. I'm not saying I won't screw up. But when I do, I'll be back on my feet. Ready to do better the next time."

In his eyes she saw no more self-deception or doubt. Only sincerity and truth.

"Think about it, okay? You don't need to answer right away."

She placed the puppy on the blanket next to the other one. Mandy was so delighted, she clapped her hands together in glee.

"I don't need to think, Nick. I know. I love you."

His smile was disbelieving at first. Then joyous. As he leaned over to kiss her, Bridget realized that she had always believed in Nick Gray. All that had been missing was for him to believe in himself, too.

* * * * *

*Mills & Boon® Special Moments™
brings you a sneak preview.*

In A Kiss To Remember *sparks fly when Nora
Simmons finds out that the Hollister house is on the
market. How dare Ben Hollister come back to
Emmett's Mill to sell his late grandparents' home
when he never came to visit them when they were alive!
Nora intends to let him know exactly what she thinks of
him...if she can only forget the kiss they once shared.*

*Turn the page for a peek at this fantastic new story
from Kimberly Van Meter, available next month in
Mills & Boon® Special Moments™!*

*Don't forget you can still find all your favourite
Superromance and Special Edition stories
every month in Special Moments™!*

A Kiss To Remember
by
Kimberly Van Meter

NORA SIMMONS DROVE past the old Victorian that sat on
the outskirts of Emmett's Mill as she went on her way
to Sonora to meet with a prospective client, and what
she saw made her stomp on the brakes and nearly eat
her steering wheel.

A sleek, shiny black import convertible sports car sat
in the driveway, completely out of place for the aging
home with its chrome wheels and leather interior,
parked as if it had a right to be there when it certainly
did not.

Sonofabitch trespassers. She made a quick U-turn,
kicking up dirt and gravel as her truck chewed up some
of the shoulder and barreled toward the house. Whoever
it was, they weren't local. Nora was willing to bet her
eyeteeth on that score. No one in Emmett's Mill drove
a BMW roadster, as far as she knew—a car like that
would stick out in the little community. Driving such a
hot little number around town was likely to drop jaws
and send a lot of die-hard American-manufacturer
purists shaking their heads in disgust. For a town in
California, Emmett's Mill had a peculiar attitude at
times.

She hopped from her truck with her cell phone in

case the sheriff was needed and prowled for the trespasser, caution at approaching a stranger barely registered. She was sick of tourists thinking that just because the town was small and quaint, the locals enjoyed having their privacy invaded. Well, B.J. and Corrinda might be dead, but Nora was not about to let a stranger wander all over their place.

She rounded the side of the expansive house and found an incredibly tall man with fashionably cut blue-black hair, with an air about him that reeked of money and privilege, examining what had at one time been Corrinda Hollister's prized roses.

Nora often found herself looking up at the opposite sex, but the breadth of his frame complemented this man's height, creating a strong, powerful build that immediately made her feel distinctly feminine. She scowled and silenced the breathless prattle in her head as she stomped toward him, purpose blotting out anything other than her own ire at his trespassing on private property.

"Can I help you?"

He turned, surprised that he wasn't alone, and no doubt the frost in her voice and the annoyed arch of one brow said volumes, as if she were the one who didn't belong on the property. "Excuse me?" he said, giving her a hard look from eyes so green they almost looked fake.

The breath caught in her throat as she met his gaze. Swallowing against the very real sensation of déjà vu, she continued in a strident tone that betrayed little of what she felt inside. "I said, can I help you? In case you weren't aware, most people don't take kindly to strangers parking in their driveway and trespassing." His per-turbed expression egged her on and she launched into him with fresh vengeance. "I happen to know the people who used to live here so don't try to say something like they were friends of yours or some other kind of bull puckey. I'll tell you what…if you just get back in your fancy car and get off the property I won't call the sheriff. Fair enough?"

"Your Mayberry Neighborhood Watch routine is cute but not necessary. I own this house."

What nerve. "Nice try, but I happen to know different," she retorted, ignoring the faint glimmer of something at the back of her brain and continuing in-dignantly. "This house belonged to—"

"B.J. and Corrinda Hollister, up until six months ago when they both died in an unfortunate car accident, leaving the house to their only grandson. Me."

The air left her lungs. Ben? She stared a little harder and although she didn't want to see it, that niggling glimmer crystallized in her memory and the image of a boy she'd kissed one summer changed into the strong facial planes of the man watching her sternly.

Oh shiza. "You're Ben Hollister?"

"It's the name on my birth certificate."

She took in the shoulders that filled his dark Henley and hinted at the solid swell of muscle hidden under-neath, and the spit dried in her mouth. Where was the skinny twelve-year-old kid with braces and his hair falling over one eye? Who was this *man?*

He turned away, dismissing her again and all she could think to say was a lame "No, you're not."

He did an annoyed double take. "I am and this is becoming irritating. Who the hell are *you?*"

She was about to jog his memory, but something—pride mainly—made her stop. She didn't consider herself a great beauty—not that she didn't catch her fair share of men looking her way—but most people said her personality made her hard to forget.

She sent him a suspicious look, but his only response was an increasingly testy glare. Either he truly didn't recognize her or he was a fabulous actor. To be fair, she looked as different as he did when they were kids. Too bad Nora wasn't in a gracious mood.

"Well, are you going to tell me who you are or not? If not, you know your way out."

Temptation to spin on her heel and do exactly that had her toes twitching but she wanted to see his reaction when she revealed her identity. Surely, her name—if not her appearance—would strike a chord, and when that burst of recognition went off like a paparazzi camera flash, she'd unleash the windstorm he'd earned for neglecting his grandparents over the years. For God's sake, the man skipped out on their funeral and now he was here surveying the property as if it were a spoil of war? What an asshole.

"Listen, I—"

"Nora Simmons," she cut in, waiting for that delicious reaction to cue her next comment, which after years of practice, had become rather scathing. But he offered very little for her to grab on to. The momentary glimmer in his eyes didn't blossom into full-blown acknowledgment as she'd hoped, but winked out in a blink and his next question was like a lawn mower over her ego.

"You're the landscape architect who did the gardens at Senator Wilkinson's lakeside estate? Near Bass Lake?" He accepted her slow nod with a smug grin that showcased each of his pearly-white, braces-free teeth, and she could only stare warily. He continued, completely missing her confusion. "How synchronistic. I was planning to call you later in the week. I never imagined you might come charging in like the Neighborhood Watch brigade, but it saves me the time of tracking you down."

Uh. What? "I…" *Twilight Zone* episode? *Punk'd?* Something wasn't right. "Wait a minute. Are you saying you don't remember me?"

"Should I?" He gave her a blank expression that looked a little too earnest to be believable and her brain started to bubble.

What game was he playing? She eyed him guardedly, deciding to see where he was going with this. "Uh, never mind. Yes, I worked on Jerry's lake house. Fun project. So, you were saying?"

"Right. I would like to hire you to fix up this place."

It was the way he said *this place* that almost ruined her ability to keep her temper in check, but her curiosity was greater than her desire to pummel him into the ground for his insensitivity, so she made an effort to cast a quick look around the craggy ridge on which the house was perched.

She took in the tall grass, star thistle and twisted

branches of manzanita of the surrounding scenery and asked, "What do you mean? What's wrong with it?"

"What's wrong with it?" he repeated incredulously. He pointed at the dead roses and the withered dry grass flanking the house that looked nothing like the beautiful oasis Corrinda had created despite the notoriously hard topsoil that, during the summer, turned to stone without constant tending. In this area of Emmett's Mill it took some skill to grow anything aside from poison oak and manzanita, but Corrinda had coaxed roses and daffodils from the difficult earth.

"Are you kidding me? It's a mess," he said. He turned a speculative eye toward her and she bristled. "Aren't you the best in the area?"

"Some seem to think so." She all but growled. Thank goodness the Hollisters never saw how their grandson had turned into such a haughty jerk. It would've broken their tender hearts.

© Kimberly Sheetz 2008

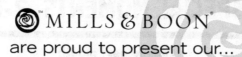

SPECIAL MOMENTS™ 2-in-1

Coming next month

SECOND-CHANCE FAMILY by Karina Bliss

The last thing workaholic Jack wants is to raise a family. But now he's guardian of his late brother's three kids. Then Jack finds out who his co-guardian is: his ex-wife, Roz!

THE OTHER SISTER by Lynda Sandoval

Paramedic Brody has been trying to come to terms with his best friend's death since high school. Can counsellor Faith help him deal with his past – and be a part of his future?

I STILL DO by Christie Ridgway

During a chance reunion in Vegas childhood sweethearts Will and Emma make good on an old pledge – to wed each other if they weren't married by thirty. Could their whim last a lifetime?

BABY BY CONTRACT by Debra Salonen

Libby is thrilled when her advertisment for a donor lands handsome Cooper Lindstrom. With his DNA, her baby will be gorgeous! But then she discovers Cooper is hiding a secret…

THE SECRET SHE KEPT by Amy Knupp

Jake had left town so fast, Savannah didn't even have time to tell him she was pregnant. When she discovers he is back in town years later, she needs to share her secret – quickly!

A KISS TO REMEMBER by Kimberly Van Meter

Nora is furious – how dare Ben return to Emmett's Mill just to sell his late grandparents' home! He will get a piece of her mind…if she can forget the kiss they once shared.

On sale 18th December 2009

Available at WHSmith, Tesco, ASDA, Eason and all good bookshops.
For full Mills & Boon range including eBooks visit
www.millsandboon.co.uk

millsandboon.co.uk Community

Join Us!

The Community is the perfect place to meet and chat to kindred spirits who love books and reading as much as you do, but it's also the place to:

- ■ **Get the inside scoop from authors about their latest books**
- ■ **Learn how to write a romance book with advice from our editors**
- ■ **Help us to continue publishing the best in women's fiction**
- ■ **Share your thoughts on the books we publish**
- ■ **Befriend other users**

Forums: Interact with each other as well as authors, editors and a whole host of other users worldwide.

Blogs: Every registered community member has their own blog to tell the world what they're up to and what's on their mind.

Book Challenge: We're aiming to read 5,000 books and have joined forces with The Reading Agency in our inaugural Book Challenge.

Profile Page: Showcase yourself and keep a record of your recent community activity.

Social Networking: We've added buttons at the end of every post to share via digg, Facebook, Google, Yahoo, technorati and de.licio.us.

www.millsandboon.co.uk

2 FREE BOOKS
AND A SURPRISE GIFT

We would like to take this opportunity to thank you for reading this Mills & Boon® book by offering you the chance to take TWO more specially selected books from the Special Moments™ series absolutely FREE! We're also making this offer to introduce you to the benefits of the Mills & Boon® Book Club™—

- **FREE home delivery**
- **FREE gifts and competitions**
- **FREE monthly Newsletter**
- **Exclusive Mills & Boon Book Club offers**
- **Books available before they're in the shops**

Accepting these FREE books and gift places you under no obligation to buy, you may cancel at any time, even after receiving your free books. Simply complete your details below and return the entire page to the address below. You don't even need a stamp!

YES Please send me 2 free Special Moments books and a surprise gift. I understand that unless you hear from me, I will receive 5 superb new stories every month, including a 2-in-1 book priced at £4.99 and three single books priced at £3.19 each, postage and packing free. I am under no obligation to purchase any books and may cancel my subscription at any time. The free books and gift will be mine to keep in any case.

Ms/Mrs/Miss/Mr _____ Initials _____

_____

Surname _____

Address _____

_____

_____ Postcode _____

Send this whole page to: Mills & Boon Book Club, Free Book Offer, FREEPOST NAT 10298, Richmond, TW9 1BR